VORTEX

"We've hit a trepidation vortex!"

. . . Gravitation tilted horribly. He went to his knees, sliding down a curve of hot steel. He fetched up brutally against a wall. Ilaloa was still with him . . .

Another globe of ball lightning hovered by. He saw a man gasping toward them. His face was hollow with terror, and he drooled from an open mouth.

The man stumbled closer. There was a knife in his hand. . . .

"Witch! Damned murdering witch, you did this!"

———————

"The shock at the end, after the action, when you suddenly realize that you've been cheering the wrong side, or the weaklings aren't, or some basic law has been ignored . . . the color, smell, taste of an alien world, a nonhuman society, a globular cluster or the universe seen from the very edge of lightspeed . . . these things Poul shows better than anyone."

—Larry Niven

———————

Books by
POUL ANDERSON

THE LONG WAY HOME
THE MAN WHO COUNTS
THE NIGHT FACE
THE PEREGRINE
QUESTION AND ANSWER
WORLD WITHOUT STARS
THE WORLDS OF POUL ANDERSON

The Saga of Dominic Flandry:
ENSIGN FLANDRY
FLANDRY OF TERRA

From Ace Science Fiction

SF

THE
PEREGRINE

by
POUL ANDERSON

SF
ace books
A Division of Charter Communications Inc.
A GROSSET & DUNLAP COMPANY
360 Park Avenue South
New York, New York 10010

THE PEREGRINE

originally published as *Star Ways*

Copyright © 1956, by Poul Anderson

INTRODUCTION

Copyright © 1978 by Poul Anderson

An ACE Book

To the MFS—all of them

Second Ace Edition: February 1978
Third Ace Edition: July 1979

Cover art by Michael Whelan

4 6 8 0 9 7 5 3
Manufactured in the United States of America

THE PEREGRINE

Introduction

Originally the title of this novel was *Star Ways*. That has been changed to avoid any appearance of exploitation of the movie *Star Wars*—which is somewhat funny, since the book has been around for more than twenty years, but may well be an improvement in its own right.

It was the third full-dress novel I wrote, following *The Broken Sword,* a fantasy, and *Vault of the Ages,* a juvenile. However, it took more than three years to see print, because the publisher who had commissioned and accepted it kept it a preposterously long time. (John Campbell, pointing out that magic is two-edged and one should never lay a curse on anybody which could harm oneself, said of this person: "May he *wish* to become ethical!") At last my agent recalled the book and placed it without another house. There a copy editor trimmed it to fit an exact number of pages, changed the name of a character because (I suppose) it looked too Russian, chopped out some very mildly erotic passages, and added silly titles to the chapters. I was not consulted about any of this, nor offered a chance to restore the original in a later paperback edition. Science fiction writers were at the bottom of the totem pole in those days, surrounded by mingent canines.

Matters have vastly improved since, and I am grateful to editor Jim Baen for a chance to fix up those of my older works which he is reissuing. In the present case, little can be done, for my copy of the manuscript has long since vanished. Fortunately, here that doesn't matter too much. The story still looks readable. It is part of a "future history" which I subsequently abandoned, but can stand independently of this. I hope you enjoy it.

—Poul Anderson

CHAPTER I

THERE IS A PLANET beyond the edge of the known, and its name is Rendezvous.

Few worlds are more lovely to the eyes of men. As the weary ships come in from space and loneliness, they see a yellow star against the great cold constellations; and nearing, they see its crowded glory swell to incandescence. The planet grows as the ships strain closer; it becomes a sapphire shield banded with clouds, blurred with rain and wind and mountain mists. The ships sweep around the planet, mooring themselves to an orbit between the moons, and it is not long before the boats spring from them and rush down out of the sky to land. And then, for a little while, the planet comes alive with noise and movement as human life spills free.

This might have been Earth, in some forgotten age before the glaciers went south. Here, there is the broad green swell of land, reaching out to a remote horizon. Far away, mountains begin; on

1

the other side is the sea. The sky is big here, lifting above the world to blue immensity.

But the difference is what haunts you. There are trees, but they are not the oak and pine and elm—or palm, baobab, sequoia—of Earth, and the wind blows through their leaves with an alien sound. The fruits of the trees are sweet, pungent, luscious to eat, but always there is the hint of a taste men never knew before. The birds are not yours; the animals of plain and forest have six legs and a greenish shimmer to their fur. At night, the constellations bear the look of strangers, and there may be four moons in the sky.

No, it is not Earth, and the knowledge becomes a hunger in you and will not let you stay. But you have never seen Earth; and by now, the hunger has become so much a part of you that you could not find a home there, either. For you are a Nomad.

And only you have learned where to find this quiet place. To all others, Rendezvous lies beyond the edge of the known.

CHAPTER II

THERE WAS nobody else on the boat. They had all swarmed off to pitch their booths and mingle with the rest, to frolic and fight and transact hard-headed business. Peregrine Joachim Henry's footsteps echoed hollow between the bare metal walls as he entered the airlock. The boat was a forty-meter column of steely comfortlessness, standing among its fellows at the end of Nomad Valley. The temporary village had mushroomed a good two kilometers from the boats.

Ordinarily, Joachim would have been down there, relaxed and genial; but he was a captain, and the Captain's Council was meeting. And this was no assembly to miss, he thought. Not with the news he had to give them.

He took the gravity shaft, floating along the upward beam to the top bunkroom where he had his box. Emerging, he crossed the floor, opened the chest. Joachim decided that a shave was in order, and ran the depilator quickly over his face.

He didn't usually bother with regalia—like all Nomads, he wore any outfit he cared to, or went nude, on a voyage. Visits to planetary surfaces didn't ordinarily require him to dress formally; but the uniform was expected of him.

"We're a hidebound bunch, really," he reflected aloud as he glanced in the mirror. It showed him a stocky man of medium height, dark-skinned, with grizzled hair and squinted gray eyes in a mesh of crow's-feet. The face was blunt and battered, crossed with deep lines, but it wasn't old. He was in early middle age—sixty-five years—but there was vitality in him.

The kilt, with its red-black-and-green Peregrine tartan, was tight around his waist. Had the damn thing shrunk? No, he was afraid he had expanded. Not much, but Jere would have kidded him about it, and let out the garment for him.

Jere. It was fifteen years now since she had made the Long Trip. And the children were grown and married. Well—He went on dressing. Over his light shirt he slipped an elaborately embroidered vest, with the Joachim coat of arms woven into the pattern. His sleeve bore the insignia of rank—captain—and service—astrogation. Buskins went on the legs; pouch and holstered gun at the waist, and plumed bonnet on the close-cropped head. Because it was hereditary and expected of him, he wore the massive gold necklace and its diamond-crusted pendant. A purple and scarlet cloak flapped over his shoulders, gauntlets on his hands.

Joachim crossed the bunkroom and went down the shaft, out the airlock, and down the retractible gangway ladder again. A dim path wound up from the valley and he took it, moving with a slightly rolling, bearlike gait. The sky was utterly blue overhead; sunlight spilled on the wide green sweep of land; wind brought him the faint crystal laughter of a bellbird. No doubt of it, man wasn't built to sit in a metal shell and hurry from star to star. It wasn't strange that so many had dropped out of Nomad life. Who had that girl been—Sean's girl, from Nerthus—?

"Salute, Hal." said a voice behind him.

He turned. "Oh Laurie. Haven't seen you for long."

Vagabond MacTeague Laurie, a walking rainbow in his uniform, fell into step beside Joachim. "Just got in yesterday," he explained. "We're the last, I suppose, and we carried word from the *Wayfarer* and the *Pilgrim* that they couldn't make it this year. So this one reckons all the ships are accounted for by now—anyway, Traveler Thorkild said he was calling the meeting for today."

"Must be. We spoke to the *Vagrant* out near Canopus, and they weren't coming. Had some kind of deal on; I suppose a new planet with trading possibilities, and they want to get there before anybody else does."

MacTeague whistled. "They're really going far afield. What were you doing out that way?"

"Just looking around," said Joachim innocently. "Nothing wrong in that. Canopus is still free territory; no ship has a claim on it yet."

"Why go on a Jump when you've got all the trade you could want right in your own territory?"

"I suppose your crew agrees with you?"

"Well, most of them. We've got some, of

course, that keep hollering for 'new horizons,' but so far they've been voted down. But—hm.'' MacTeague's eyes narrowed. ''If you've been prowling around Canopus, Hal, then there's money out there.''

The Captains' Hall stood near the edge of a bluff. More than two centuries ago, when the Nomads found Rendezvous and chose it for their meeting place, they had raised the Hall. Two hundred years of rain, wind, and sunlight had fled; and still the Hall was there. It might be standing when all the Nomads were gone into darkness.

Man was a small and hurried thing; his spaceships spanned the light-years, and his feverish death-driven energy made the skies of a thousand worlds clangorous with his works—but the old immortal dark reached farther than he could imagine.

The other captains were also arriving, a swirl of color and a rumble of voices. There were only about thirty this rendezvous—four ships had reported they wouldn't be coming, and then there were the missing ones. The captains were all past their youth, some of them quite old.

Each Nomad ship was actually a clan—an exogamous group claiming a common descent. There were, on the average, some fifteen hundred people of all ages belonging to each vessel, with women marrying into their husbands' ships. The captaincy was hereditary, each successor being elected from the men in that family, if any were qualified.

But names cut across ships. There had only

been sixteen families in the *Traveler I*, which had started the whole Nomad culture, and adoption had not added a great many more. Periodically, when the vessels grew overcrowded, the younger people would get together and found a new one, with all the Nomads helping to build them a ship. That was the way the fleet had expanded. But the presidency of the Council was hereditary with the Captain of the *Traveler*—third of that name in the three hundred years since the undying voyage began—and he was always a Thorkild.

Wanderer, Gypsy, Hobo, Voyageur, Bedouin, Swagman, Trekker, Explorer, Troubadour, Adventurer, Sundowner, Migrant—Joachim watched the captains go in, and wondered at the back of his mind what the next ship would do for a name. There was a tradition which forbade using a name not taken from some human language.

When everyone else had entered, Joachim mounted the porch himself and walked into the Hall. It was a big and goodly place, its pillars and paneling carved with intricate care, hung with tapestries and polished metal reliefs. Whatever you could say against the Nomads, you had to admit they were good at handicrafts.

Joachim sank into his chair at the table, crossed his legs, and fumbled for his pipe. By the time he had lit up and was emitting cheerful blue clouds, Traveler Thorkild Helmuth was calling the meeting to order. Thorkild was a tall, gaunt, and stern-faced man, white of hair and beard, stiffly erect in his carved darkwood seat.

"In the name of Cosmos, rendezvous," he began formally. Joachim didn't pay much attention to the ritual that followed.

"All ships except five are now present or accounted for," concluded Thorkild, "and therefore I call this meeting to discuss facts, determine policy, and make proposals to lay before the voters. Has anyone a matter to present?"

There was, as usual, quite a bit, none of it very important. The *Romany* wanted a territory extending fifty light-years about Thossa to be recognized as her own—no other Nomad ship to trade, exploit, build, organize, or otherwise make use of said region without permission of the assignee. This was on grounds of the *Romany's* having done most of the exploration thereabouts. After some discussion, that was granted.

The *Adventurer* wished to report that the Shan of Barjaz-Kaui on Davenigo, otherwise known as Ettalume IV, had laid a new tax on traders. The planet being known to the Coordination Service, it wasn't possible for Nomads to overthrow the Shar by violence, but with some help it might be possible to subvert his government and get a friendlier prince. Was anyone interested? Well, the *Bedouin* might be; they could talk it over later.

The *Stroller* had had more direct difficulties with the Cordys. It seemed the ship had been selling guns to a race who weren't supposed to be ready for such technology, and Coordination Service had found out about it. All Nomads had better watch their step for a while.

The *Fiddlefoot* was going to Spica, where she intended to barter for Solarian products, and wanted to know if anyone cared to buy a share in her enterprise. Goods hauled clear from Sol were expensive.

It went on—proposal, debate, argument, report, ultimate decision. Joachim yawned and scratched himself. His chance came finally, and he flicked a finger upward. "Captain Peregrine Joachim," acknowledged Thorkild. "Do you speak for your ship?"

"For myself and a few others," said Joachim, "but my ship will follow me in this. I've got a report to make."

"Proceed."

Then eyes turned on him, down the length of the Council table.

Joachim began recharging his pipe. "This one has been sort of curious for the last few years," he said, "and he's been keeping his eyes open. You might think I was a Cordy, the way I've been reconstructing the crime. And I think it is a crime, or maybe a war. A quiet but very thorough war." He paused calculatingly to light his tobacco. "In the past ten years or so, we've lost five ships. They never reported back to anyone. What does that mean? It could happen once or twice by sheer accident, but you know how careful we are in dealing with the unknown. Five ships is just too many to lose. Especially when we lose them all in the same region."

"Now hold on, Captain Peregrine," said Thorkild. "That isn't so. Those ships disappeared in the direction of Sagittari—but that includes a hell of a lot of space. Their courses wouldn't have come within many parsecs of each other."

"No-o-o. Maybe not. Still, the Union covers even more territory than this volume of space where our people vanished."

"Are you implying—No, that's ridiculous. Many other ships have been through that region without coming to harm, and they report that it's completely uncivilized. Such planets as we touched at have been thoroughly backward. Not a mechanical culture on even one of them."

"Uh-huh." Joachim nodded. "Isn't that an odd fact? In so big a chunk of space, there should be some race which has at least gotten as far as steam engines."

"Well, we've touched on—hm." Thorkild stroked his beard.

Romany Ortega Pedro, who had a photographic memory, spoke up. "The volume within which those ships disappeared is, let us say, twenty or thirty million cubic light-years. It contains perhaps four million suns, of which virtually all are bound to have planets. It's an unpromising region precisely because it is so backward, and few ships have gone there. To my knowledge, Nomads have stopped at less than a thousand stars in that volume. Now really, Joachim, you consider that a fair sample?"

"No. I just mention it as a little—indication, shall we say? I repeat, this one denies that five ships in ten years could have been lost because of unknown diseases, treacherous natives, trepidation vortices, or the like. Their captains weren't that stupid.

"I've talked with Nomads who've been there, and also with outsiders—explorers, traders,

scouts looking for colony sites, anyone. Or anything, since I also got hold of some otherlings"
—he meant nonhuman spacemen—"who had passed through or stopped by. I even talked my way into the Cordy office on Nerthus, and got a look at their Galactic Survey records.

"Space is too big. Even this little splinter of the Galaxy that man has traversed is larger than we can think—and we've spent our lives in the void. It's thirty thousand light-years to Galactic center. There are some *hundred billion* suns in the Galaxy! Man will never be able to think concretely in such terms. It just can't be done.

"So a lot of information lies around in the shape of isolated facts, and nobody coordinates it and sees what the facts mean. Even the Service can't do it—they have troubles enough running the Union without worrying about the frontiers and the beyond-frontiers. When I started investigating, I found I was the first being who'd even thought of this."

"And what," asked Thorkild quietly, "have you found out?"

"Not too much, but it's damned indicative. There have been otherling ships which vanished in that region, too. But Coordination and Survey never had any trouble. If something had happened to one of *their* vessels, they'd have spyboats out there so fast they'd meet themselves coming back. You see what it means? *Somebody* knows a lot about our civilization—enough to know who it's safe to molest.

"Then there are any number of E-planets—which is what you'd expect—and not too many of them seem to have natives—which is what you wouldn't expect. They—well, there are at least a dozen which remind you of Rendezvous, beautiful green worlds with not a building or a road in sight.''

''Maybe they're shy, like the ones on this planet,'' said Vagabond MacTeague. ''We'd been here for fifty years before we knew there were natives. And a similar case happened on Nerthus, you remember.''

''The Nerthusians have an unusual sort of culture,'' said Romany Ortega thoughtfully. ''No, most likely those worlds you speak of are really inhabited.''

''All right,'' said Joachim. ''There's more to tell. In a few cases, there were E-planets with what we'd considered a normal culture: houses, farming, and so on. Contact was made rather easily in all those instances, and in general the natives seemed not unfamiliar with the sight of space-ships. But when I checked the reports against each other, I found that none of those planets had been visited before by anyone from *our* civilization.''

''Now hold on,'' began Thorkild. ''You aren't suggesting—''

''There's more yet.'' Joachim interrupted. ''Unfortunately, few scientifically minded expeditions have been in the—the X region, so I couldn't get an accurate description of flora and fauna. However, a couple of those I talked to had been struck by what seemed remarkably similar plants and trees on some of these supposedly uninhabited E-planets. Galactic Survey had some helpful information there. They had noted more than similarity—they had found *identity* of a good dozen plant species on six uninhabited worlds. Explain that away!''

''How did Survey explain it?'' asked Fiddlefoot Kogama.

''They didn't. Too much else to do. Their robotfile had integrated a reasonable probability that the similarity was due to transplantation, maybe accidental, by a Tiunran expedition.''

''Tiunra? I don't think I've heard—''

''Probably you wouldn't have. They're the natives of an M-planet on the other side of Vega. Strange culture—they had space travel a good five hundred years before man left Sol, but they never were interested in colonization. Even today, I understand they don't have much to do with the Union. They're just uninterested.

''Anyway, I took the trouble to write to Tiunra. Sent the letter off on Nerthus a good two years ago. I asked whoever was in charge of their survey records about the X region. What had they found out? What had been done by them, or to them, out here?

''I got my answer six months ago, when we stopped back at Nerthus. Very polite; they'd even written in human Basic. Yes, their ships had gone through the X region about four centuries ago. But they hadn't noticed the things I mentioned, and were sure they hadn't done any transplanting, accidentally or otherwise. And *they* had lost four ships.

''All right.'' Joachim leaned back, sprawling his

legs under the table, and blew a series of smoke rings. "There you have it, lads. Make what you will of it."

Silence, then. The wind blowing in through the open door stirred the tapestries. A light metal plaque rang like a tiny gong.

Finally Ortega spoke, as if with an effort: "What about the Tiunrans? Didn't they do anything about their missing ships?"

"No, except leave this part of space alone," said Joachim.

"And they haven't informed Coordination?"

"Not as far as I know. But then, Coordination never asked them."

Thorkild looked bleak. "This is a serious matter."

"Now there's an understatement," drawled Joachim.

"You haven't absolutely proved your case."

"Maybe not. But it sure ought to be looked into."

"Very well, then. Let's accept your guess. The X region, perhaps the entire Great Cross, is under the rule of a secretive and hostile civilization technologically equal to ours—or superior, for all we know. I still can't imagine how you'd conceal the kind of technology involved. Just consider the neutrino emission of a large atomic power plant, for instance. You can find your way across many light-years to a planet where they're using atomic energy, just by the help of a neutrino detector. Well, maybe they have some kind of screen." Thorkild tapped the table with a lean forefinger. "So, they don't like us and they've spied us out a bit. What does that imply?''

"Conquest—they figure to invade the Union?" asked MacTeague.

Trekker Petroff said, "They may just want to be left alone."

"What could they hope to gain by war?" protested Ortega.

"I'm not guessing about motives," said Joachim. "Those creatures aren't human. I say we'd better assume they're hostile."

"All right," said Thorkild. "You've given most thought to this business. What follows?"

"Why, look at the map," said Joachim mildly. "The Union, both as a cultural and a semipolitical unit, is expanding inward toward Galactic center, Sagittari. The X empire lies squarely across the Union's path. X, however peaceful, may feel that countermeasures are called for.

"And where are *we?* On the Sagittari-ward frontier of the Union, and spreading into the unmapped regions beyond. Right smack between the Union and X. The Coordination Service of the Union doesn't like Nomads, and X has already shown what he thinks of us. We're the barbarians—right between the upper and nether millstones!"

Another pause. Death they could face, but extinction of their entire tribe was a numbing concept; and the whole Nomad history had been one long flight from cultural absorption.

Thirty-odd ships, with some fifty thousand humans—*what can be done?*

Joachim answered the unspoken cry with a few slow words:

"I've been thinking about this for some little

while, friends, and have some sort of an answer. The first requirement of any operation is intelligence, and we don't even know if X *is* a menace.

"Here's what this one proposes. Let's just keep the matter quiet for the time being. Naturally, no ship will enter the Great Cross, but otherwise we can go on as usual. But I'll make a scout of the *Peregrine*, and we'll spy out the unknowns."

"Eh?" Thorkild blinked at him.

"Sure. I'll tell most of my crew, at first, that it's an exploratory venture. We'll snoop around as we ordinarily do, and I'll direct the snooping the way I think'll be most useful. We can fight if we must, and once we go into hyperdrive we can't be followed or shot at."

"Well, that sounds—very good," said Thorkild.

"Of course," smiled the Peregrine, "we can't be hampered in our work. I'll want a formal action-in-council authorizing me or my crew to break, bend, or even obey any law of the Nomads, the Union, or anybody else that may seem convenient."

"Hmmm—I think I see where this could lead," said MacTeague.

"Also," said Joachim blandly, "the *Peregrine* will be in a primitive region—and hostile where it's not primitive—and won't have the normal chance to turn an honest credit. We'll want a—say a twenty percent share in all profits made between now and next rendezvous."

"*Twenty percent!*" choked Ortega.

"Sure. We're risking our whole ship, aren't we?"

CHAPTER III

PEREGRINE THORKILD SEAN could not forget the girl who had stayed behind on Nerthus. She had gone alone into the city, Stellamont, and had not come back. After a while, he had taken a flier and gone the twelve hundred kilometers to her father's home. There was no hope—she couldn't endure the Nomad life.

Two years can be a long time, and memories blur. Thorkild Sean walked through the Nomad camp under the heaven of Rendezvous and knew how far away Nerthus was.

Darkness had come to the valley—not the still shadow of Nerthus, which was almost another Earth, but the living, shining night of Rendezvous. Fires burned high, and the camp was one babel. The trading had gone on till it was done. The Captains' Council had met, and its proposals had been voted on by the men of the ships—now the time of rendezvous was ready to culminate in the Mutiny. Unmarried women were not allowed to attend that three-day saturnalia—the Nomads were strict with their maidens—but for everyone else it would be a colorful memory to take skyward.

Except for me, thought Sean.

He passed a bonfire, crossing the restless circle of its light—a tall slender young man, fair-skinned, brown-haired, blue-eyed, his face thin and mobile, his movements angular and loose-jointed.

Somebody hailed him, but he ignored it and went on his way. Not tonight, not tonight. Presently the camp was behind him. He found the trail he was looking for and followed it steeply upward out of the dale. The night of Rendezvous closed in on him.

This was not Earth, nor was it Nerthus, or any other planet where men had built their homes. He could walk free here, and no hidden menace of germ or mold or poisoned tooth waited for him; yet somehow Sean felt that he had never been on so foreign a world.

Three moons were up. One was a far white shield, cold in the velvet sky; the second a glowing amber crescent, and the third almost full and hurtling between the stars so that he could see it moving. Three shadows followed him over the long, whispering grass, and one of them moved by itself. The light was so bright that the shadows were not black; they were a dusky blue on the moon-frosted ground.

Overhead were the stars, constellations unknown to the home of humanity. The Milky Way was still there, a bridge of light, and he could see the cold brilliance of Spica and Canopus, but most of heaven was strange.

The hills into which he went stirred with moonlight and shadow. Forest lifted on one side of his path, high feathery-leaved trees overgrown with blossoming vines. On the other side there was grass and bush and lonely copse. Now and then he saw one of the six-legged animals of Rendezvous. None of them were afraid; it was as if they knew he wasn't going to shoot at them.

Light moved here and there. The glowing insects bobbed on frail wings over the phosphorescent glow of lamp-flowers. Sean let the sounds of the night flow into him. The memory of his wife drowned as if in rippling water, and the new eagerness within him was a quiet, steady burning.

She stood where she had told him to come, leaning against a tree and watching him stride across the hills. His footsteps grew swifter until he was running.

The Nomads had looked for an Earthlike planet—E-planet—outside of the ordinary space lanes, a meeting place which no others would be likely to find. They had not explored much beyond the site chosen for their gatherings, but even so it had been a shock, fifty years later, when they learned that Rendezvous had natives after all. The laws on the Union were of small concern, but aborigines could mean trouble.

These dwellers had been a gentle sort, though, remarkably humanoid but possessing a culture unlike any ever created by man. They had sought out the newcomers, had learned the Nomad dialect with ease, and had asked many questions. But they had not told much concerning themselves;

nor were the Nomads especially interested, once it became clear that these beings had nothing to trade.

The natives had courteously presented the Nomads with the area they already held, only that they not be molested elsewhere, and this the humans had readily voted into law. Since then, an occasional native had shown up at the assemblies, to watch for a while and disappear again—nothing else, for a good hundred and fifty years.

Blind, thought Sean. *We're blind as man has always been. There was a time when he imagined he was the only intelligent life in the universe—and he hasn't changed much.*

The thought died in the wonder that stood before him. He stopped, and the noise of his heart was loud in his ears. "Ilaloa."

She stood looking at him, not moving or speaking. The loveliness of her caught at his throat.

She could have been human—almost—had she not been so unhumanly fair. The Lorinyans were what man might be in a million years of upward evolution. Their bodies were slim and full of a liquid grace, marble-white; the hair on their heads was like silk, floating about the shoulders and down the back, the color of blued silver. He had first seen Ilaloa when the *Peregrine* came to Rendezvous and he had wandered off to be alone.

"I came, Ilaloa," he said, feeling the clumsiness of words. She remained quiet, and he sighed and sat down at her feet.

He didn't have to talk to her. With men, he was a lonely being, forever locked into the night of his own skull, crying to his kindred and never knowing them or feeling their nearness. Language was a bridge and a barrier alike, and Sean knew that men talk because they are afraid to be silent. But with Ilaloa he could know quiet; there was understanding and no loneliness.

Let the native females be! It was Nomad law which needed little enforcement on other planets—who was attracted by something that looked like a caricature of man? But no spear had thudded into his flesh when he met this being who was not less but more than a woman; and there had, after all, been nothing to disgrace them.

Ilaloa sat down beside him. He looked at her face—the smooth, lovely planes and curves of it, arched brows over huge violet eyes, small tilted nose, delicate mouth.

"When do you leave?" she asked. Her voice was low, richly varied.

"In three days," he answered. "Let's not talk about it."

"But we should," she said gravely. "Where will you go?"

"Out." He waved his hand at the thronging stars. "From sun to sun, I don't know where. It will be into new territory this time, I hear."

"To there?" She pointed at the Great Cross.

"Why—yes. Toward Sagittari. How did you know?"

She smiled. "We hear talk, even in the forest. Will you come back, Sean?"

"If I live. But it won't be for at least two years—a little more in your reckoning. Maybe four years, or six, I don't know." He tried to grin. "By then, Ilaloa, you will be—whatever your

21

people do, and have children of your own."

"Have you none, Sean?"

It was the most natural thing in the universe to tell her of what had happened. She nodded seriously and laid her fingers across his.

"How lonely you must be." There was no sentimentality in her voice; it was almost matter-of-fact. But she understood.

"I get along," he said. With a sudden rising of bitterness: "But I don't want to speak of going away. That will happen all too soon."

"If you do not want to leave," she said, "then stay."

He shook his head heavily. "No. It's impossible. I couldn't stay, even on a planet of my own kind. For three hundred years the Nomads have been living between the stars. Those who couldn't endure it dropped out, and those from the planets who fitted into our kind of life were taken in. Don't you see, it's more even than habit and culture by now. We've been bred for this."

"I know," she said. "I only wanted to make it clear in your own mind."

"I'm going to miss you," he told her. His words stumbled over each other. "I don't dare think how much I'll miss you, Ilaloa."

"You have only known me for some few days."

"It seems longer—or shorter—I don't know. Never mind. Forget it. I've no right to say some things."

"Maybe you do," she answered.

He turned around, looking at her, and the night was wild with the sudden clamor of his heart.

CHAPTER IV

"YOU WILL GO to the Sagittarian frontier of the Stellar Union," the machine had said. "The planet Carsten's Star III, otherwise called Nerthus, is recommended as a starting point. Thereafter—"

The directive had been general and left the agent almost complete discretion. Theoretically, he was free to refuse. But if he had been the sort to do that, Trevelyan Micah would not have been a field agent of the Stellar Union Coordination Service in the first place.

The psychology of it was complex. The Cordy agents were in no sense swashbucklers, and they knew the fear of death often enough to realize that there was nothing glamorous about it. They believed their work to be valuable, but were not especially altruistic. Perhaps one could say that they loved the work.

His aircar went on soundless gravity beams over the western half of North America. The land was big and green below him, forest and rivers and grass waving out to the edge of the world. Scattered homes reflected sunlight, upward, isolated houses and small village groupings. Though, in a way, all Earth was a city by now, he thought. When transportation and communication make any spot on the planet practically next door, and the whole is a socioeconomic unity, that world is a city—with half a billion people in it!

The sky was full of aircraft, gleaming ovoids against the high blue. Trevelyan let his autopilot steer him through the fourth-level traffic and sat back smoking a thoughtful cigarette. There was a lot of movement on and over Earth these days. Few were ever really still; you couldn't be, if you had a job in Africa and a—probably temporary— dwelling in South America, and were planning a holiday at Arctic Resort with your Australian and Chinese friends. Even the interstellar colonists, deliberately primitive though they were, tended to scatter themselves across their planets.

There had been no economic reason for the outward surge of man when the hyperdrive was invented; the emigration was a mute revolt of people for whom civilization no longer had any need. They wanted to be of use, wanted something greater than themselves to which they could devote their lives—if it were only providing a living for themselves and their children. Cybernetic society had taken that away from them. If you weren't in the upper ten percent—a scientist, or an artist of more than second-rate talent—there was nothing you could do which a machine couldn't do better.

So they moved out. It had not happened overnight, nor had it fully happened yet. But the balance had shifted, both socially and genetically. And a planet, the bulk of whose population was creative, necessarily controlled the intangibles that in the long run would shape all society. There was scientific research; there was the education that directs men's thoughts, and the art that colors them. There was above all an understanding of the whole huge turbulent process.

Trevelyan's thoughts ended as the autopilot buzzed a signal. He was approaching the Rocky Mountains now, and Diane's home was near.

It was a small unit perched almost on the Continental Divide. Around it, the mountains rose white and colossal, and overhead the sky was pale with cold. When Trevelyan stepped out, the chill struck like a knife through his thin garments. He ran to the door, which scanned him as he neared and opened for him, and shivered once he was inside.

"Diane!" he exclaimed. "You choose the damnedest places to live. Last year it was the Amazon Basin. . . . When are you moving to Mars?"

"When I want to multiplex it," she said. "Hullo, Micah."

Her casual voice was belied by the kiss she gave him. She was a small woman, with something young and wistful about her.

"New project?"

"Yes. Coming along pretty well too. I'll show you." She touched keys on the multiplex and the tape began its playback. Trevelyan sat down to absorb the flow of stimuli-color patterns, music, traces of scent and associated taste. It was abstract, but it called up before him the mountains and all mountains which had ever been.

"It's good," he said. "I felt as if I were ten kilometers up on the edge of a glacier."

"You're too literal," she answered, stroking his hair. "This is supposed to be a generalized impression. I'd like to work in some genuine cold, but that's too distracting. I have to settle for things like ice-blue color and treble notes."

"And you say you never learned the cybernetic theory of art?"

" 'Art is a form of communication,' " she quoted in a singsong. " 'Communication is the conveyance of information. Information is a pattern in space-time, distinguished by rules of selection from the totality of all possible arrangements of the same constituents, and thus capable of being assigned a meaning. Meaning is the induced state of the percipient and in the case of art is primarily emotional—' Bother it! You can have your mathematical logic. I know what works and what doesn't, and that's enough."

It was, he realized. Braganza Diane might not grasp the synthesizing world-view of modern philosophy, but it didn't matter. She created.

"You should have let me know you were coming, Micah," she said. "I'd have made arrangements."

"I didn't know it myself until just lately. I've been called back. I came to say goodbye."

She sat quiet for a long moment. When she spoke, it was very low, and she was looking away from him: "It couldn't wait?"

"I'm afraid not. It's rather urgent."

"Where are you going?"

"Sagittari frontier. After that anything can happen."

"Damn," she said between her teeth. "Damn and triple damn."

"I'll be back," he said.

"Someday," she answered thinly, "you won't come back." Then, getting to her feet: "Well, relax. You can stay tonight, of course? Good, let's have a drink now."

She fetched wine in goblets of Lunar crystal. He clinked glasses with her, listening to the faint clear belling, and raised his to the light before he drank. A ruby flame glowed in its heart.

"Good," he said appreciatively. "What's the news from your end?"

"Nothing. There's never very much, is there? Well, I had an offer from an admirer. He even wanted a contract."

"If he's a right sort," said Trevelyan gravely, "I think you should take him up on it."

She regarded him where he sat, and saw a big, lean man, his body compact and balanced with the training of modern education. His face was dark and hook-nosed, a deep wrinkle between the green eyes, and most people would have called the light of those eyes cold. The hair was straight and black, with a reddish tint where the sun caught it. There was something ageless and impassive about him.

Well—the Coordination Service caught its agents young. They weren't supermen; they were something less understandable.

"No," she said. "I won't."

"It's your life." He didn't press the matter.

Their liaison went back several years. For him,

she knew, it was a pleasant convenience, nothing more; he had not offered a contract and she had not asked for one.

"What is your directive this time?" she asked.

"I don't know, really. That's the worst of it."

"You mean the machine wouldn't tell you?"

"The machine didn't know."

"But that's impossible!"

"No, it isn't. It's happened before, and it will happen again with increasing frequency until—" Trevelyan scowled. "The real problem is finding some new principle altogether. It might even be philosophical, for all I know."

"I don't understand."

"Look," he said, "the basis of civilization is communication. In fact, life itself depends on communication and feedback loops between organism and environment, and between parts of the same organism.

"Now consider what we have today. There are approximately a million stars which have been visited by man, and the number grows almost daily. Many of these stars have one or more planets inhabited by beings of intelligence comparable to ours, but often with action-and-thought patterns so different that only long, painstaking study will ever suggest their fundamental motivation. Full empathy remains impossible. Imagine the effects on these of a sudden introduction to an interstellar civilization! We have to reckon with their future as well as our own.

"Remember your history, Diane. Think what happened in Earth's past when there were sovereign states working at unintegrated cross-purposes.''

''You needn't strain the obvious,'' she said, annoyed.

''Sorry. I'm just trying to tie in the general background. It's fantastically complex, and the problem is getting worse. It's a case of transportation outstripping communication. We've *got* to bring all the components of our civilization together. You need only recall what happened on Earth back around the Second Dark Ages. Nowadays it could happen between whole stellar systems!''

She was still for a moment, throwing away one cigarette and lighting another. ''Sure,'' she said, then. ''That's what the Union was organized to prevent. That's what Cordy work consists of.''

''We've found different types and emphases of intelligence in the Galaxy,'' he flung at her, ''but they can all be given a rating on the same general scale. Ever wondered why there is no species whose average intelligence is appreciably higher than man's?''

''Why—well, aren't all the planets about the same age?''

''Not that close. A million or ten million years should make a real difference to organic life. No, Diane, it's a matter of natural limits. The nervous system, especially the brain, can only become so complex, then the whole thing gets too big to control itself.''

''I think I see what you're driving at,'' she said. ''There are natural limits to the capacities of computing machines, too.''

"Uh-huh. Also to systems made up of many machines together. Diane, we can't coordinate as many planets as are included in our civilization-range today. And that range is still expanding."

She nodded. Her face was serious, and there was a foreboding in the eyes that met his. "You're right—but what does this have to do with your new mission?"

"The overworked integrators are years behind in correlating information," he said. "A thing can grow to monstrous proportions before they learn of it. And we, the flesh-and-blood Cordys, are no better off. We perform our missions, but we can't oversee *everything*. The integrator has finally gotten around to considering some reports of disappearing ships, botanical anomalies on supposedly uninhabited planets, and the Nomad clans. The probability indicates something tremendous."

"What is that?" she breathed.

"I don't know," he answered. "The machine suggested that the Nomads might be up to something. I'm going to find out."

"Why do you Cordys have it in for the poor Nomads so much?"

"They're the worst disruptive factor our civilization has," he said grimly. "They go everywhere and do anything, with no thought of the consequences. To Earth, the Nomads are romantic wanderers; to me, they're a pain.

"I doubt that they're behind this business. I suspect something much more significant." He took out a cigarette and put it to his lips. "But the Nomads will make a handy place to start."

CHAPTER V

"NO!"

Thorkild Sean looked into his father's eyes. "I don't see what you have to say about it."

"Are you out of your mind?" Thorkild Elof shook his head like an angry bull. The beard and the maned hair of a ship elder swirled white about his shoulders. "I'm your *father*."

Something in Sean stirred then. Ilaloa's fingers closed taut around his. Looking down, he saw fear in the big violet eyes, and remembered how far apart he and Elof had grown in the last four years. He straightened his shoulders. "I'm a free crewman of the Nomads, and I do as I please."

"We'll see about that!" Elof swung about, lifting his voice. "Hal! Hal, come over here, will you?"

Joachim Henry stood watching the people of his ship file into their boats. It was a long straggling line—men still disheveled and hilarious from the Mutiny. The married women proceeded with careful dignity, most of them holding babies; the younger girls and boys looked wistfully back at the valley.

"Sean," whispered Ilaloa. He tightened his arm about her slender waist, feeling her tremble. The long silver hair streamed wildly from her head—with its fine clean molding and white skin and enormous eyes. But he felt the terror deep within her.

Joachim heard Elof's shout. "Now what?" he grumbled. He gave his kilt a hitch and strolled to the argument.

"Hello, Elof, Sean," he nodded. "Who's the—" He caught himself. "The native lady?"

"This is Ilaloa." Sean's voice was strained. Joachim's eyes lingered appreciatively on the female.

"What d'you want?" He gestured with his pipestem at the line of embarkees. "I got enough to do, nursing them back onto the ship. Make it short, will you, lads?"

"It can be," said Elof. "Sean here wants to take this native along. He wants to *marry* her!"

"Eh?" Joachim's eyes narrowed in a mesh of fine wrinkles. "Now Sean, you know the law."

"We're not offending native notions," the boy threw back at him. "Ilaloa is free to come with me if she wants."

"Your father?" Joachim spoke softly to her. "Your tribe? What do they have to say?"

"I am free," she answered. Her tones were the sweetest sound he had heard in a long time. "We have no—tribes. Each of us is free."

"Well—" Joachim rubbed his chin.

"What's going on here?"

It was a woman's voice, low and even, and Joachim turned to the newcomer with a feeling of relief. If he could let them argue it out to a decision of their own, perhaps he could keep clear of the mess.

Besides, he liked Nicki.

She walked up to them with the long swinging stride that was a challenge in itself. She was blonde, as tall as many men, and strongly built; there was a supple flow of muscles under her smooth, pale-gold skin. She walked over to her brother-in-law and looked into his troubled countenance. "What's wrong, Sean?"

A slow smile of greeting lifted his mouth. "It's Ilaloa," he said. "We want to go with the ship— together."

Nicki's blue-eyed gaze locked with the infinite violet of the Lorinyan's. Then she smiled and clapped a hand on the slim white shoulder. "Be welcome, Ilaloa," she said. "Sean's been needing somebody like you."

If proof had been required, Joachim would have considered that sufficient to destroy the malicious gossip about Sean and Nicki. Landlouper Mac-Teague Nicki had been eighteen, an average Nomad age for marriage, when her father and Elof arranged for her to wed Sean's younger brother Einar. The alliance had been tempestuous; then a landslide on Vixen killed Einar.

His widow was left in an anomalous position, a Peregrine and Thorkild by virtue of marriage, but without children to bind her to the family. Normally, Elof would have acted as her father and arranged another husband for her, but she had rejected the whole idea with an almost physical violence. She lived man-fashion, working for herself as a weaver and potter, and even doing her own trading on planets they visted. And the most irritating part of it, as far as the community was concerned, was that she did very well.

After his own divorce, two years ago, Sean had moved in with Nicki. They had separate rooms and respected each other's privacy. Under Nomad law, marriage was forbidden to them as members of the same ship; and tongues had been wagging ever since.

Elof drew him aside. "The boy's soft in the head, skipper," he said. "Throw the law at him. He'll get over it."

"Hm. I wonder." Joachim looked slantwise at the older Thorkild. "What's the background on this?"

"Well, you know how he tumbled for that Nerthusian wench. I didn't like it, but I didn't want to press him too far, either. She wasn't such a bad sort anyway, for a settler, until she deserted him. But since then—well, you know how Sean's been. Nobody can get along with him except Nicki, and that's bad—don't either of them have any sense of decency? Then the boy disappears this rendezvous, hardly shows himself, and I was all prepared to get him a nice wife from the Trekker Petroffs, too. And now he shows up with *this!*"

"Well," said Joachim mildly, "he's been married once. That makes him legally an adult."

"You know the law, Hal. And you know the biology of it, too. Different species can't interbreed. There'd be no children—only trouble.''

Yes, thought Joachim glumly, *there'd be that all right. And what do we really know about this race?*

''There's plenty of room in Sean's and my quarters,'' said Nicki to Ilaloa. ''We'll get along fine.''

''A native can't be married, and she can't be adopted,'' snapped Elof.

Sean's face was white and stiff. ''Ilaloa can be useful, Skipper. I think her people are telepaths.''

''Eh?'' Joachim blinked at him. The word was blown down the wind and a man halted—then moved slowly away.

''Is that so?'' the captain asked the Lorinyan.

''I do not know,'' she answered. The fine hair stirred about her thin-carved face as if it had life of its own. ''Sometimes we know things even about you. I have no word for it, but we can—feel?''

''There haven't been any natives around at this rendezvous,'' said Sean eagerly, ''but Ilaloa knew the *Peregrine* was going into the Great Cross. A telepath in any degree can be a big help.''

Or a big grief, thought Joachim. He puffed his pipe back into furious life and let his eyes rest on the Thorkilds. Ilaloa interested him. If what she said was true, that her people wouldn't make difficulties over her removal—and he had to assume that much—she might indeed have her uses. Neurosensitivity in any degree was not a gift to be despised.

''Let's be reasonable about this,'' he said. ''We don't want a break in the family, Elof.''

''The captain is the judge,'' answered the older man coldly, ''but you've bent the law enough in the past.''

"Well, Sean," said Joachim, "of course you can't marry her. The law's quite plain on that. However, there's nothing to forbid you"—he grinned slyly—"keeping a pet."

He had thought Ilaloa would take offense, but she laughed now, a sudden joyous peal, and one arm went about Sean. "Thank you," she said. "Thank you."

Sean looked rattled, but Nicki chuckled.

"Nothing to thank this one for," said Joachim. "I just interpret the law.

"Dad—" Sean spoke timidly. "Dad, when you get to know her—"

"Never mind." Thorkild Elof turned and walked away, his head unnaturally high. Joachim looked after him with a tinge of pity. It was hard on the old man. His wife was dead, his daughters married and out of the family, one son was gone and the other had raised a wall between them. *I know how lonesome a man can get,* Joachim thought.

"I reckon that settles it," said the captain. "Get busy, Sean. We have stuff to load aboard." He sauntered back to the embarkation.

"Nice work," said Nicki. "And welcome again, Ilaloa."

Sean and Ilaloa looked at each other. "You can come with me," said the man wonderingly, not quite believing it yet. "You *will* come."

"Yes," she said.

She looked across the valley; it was as if she listened to the windy roar of trees and the remote shouting of the sea. A shiver went through her and she covered her face briefly. Then she turned again to Sean and her voice seemed to come from very far away: ''Let us be going.''

He held her close for a moment, then they walked hand in hand toward the boats.

CHAPTER VI

THE ECONOMY of the frontier planets, and therefore the physical arrangement of their artifacts, is as different from Earth's as the rest of their culture. Like most new lands of human history, they show a reversion to older and more primitive types of social organization; yet it is not a reconstruction of the past which exists there.

From Sol to the vaguely defined Sagittari frontier of the Union was a two months' voyage even in the fastest hyperdrive transport. But the Solarian's own needs were adequately provided for at home; he had no particular reason to haul goods out to the stars. The interstellar colonists had to provide for themselves.

They scattered over the faces of many planets, those colonists. They weren't isolated, not with their telescreens and gravity fliers, but they dwelt well apart. A small but brisk trade went on between the stars of any given sector, carried by merchant ships or by such Nomads as weren't heading out into the depthless yonder. A few goods from Sol itself, or other highly civilized systems, found their way out to the frontier, too. That meant spaceports, warehouses, depots, service and repair establishments, shops—and with them, local robot factories, entertainment facilities, and administrative centers. The city, a forgotten phenomenon of Solar history, was reborn.

One for a planet, or even a system, was usually enough. The city on Carsten's Star III, Nerthus, was called Stellamont. Joachim brought the *Peregrine* there to get supplies and ammunition.

The trip took about three weeks.

The *Peregrine* contacted Nerthus' robot monitor, and was assigned an orbit about the world. Her visit was to be short, so most of the crew were left aboard; Joachim and a few assistants went "down" in a couple of fliers to dicker, and a boat took a single liberty party, chosen by lot. The rest swore philosophically and carried on with their usual shipboard rounds. Among other things, the *Peregrine* had a poker and a dice game in the main recreation room which, with interruptions, had been going so long—about a century now—that their continuance had become almost a fetish.

Joachim had based his success in the captaincy on a number of tricks, among them the fine art of rigging lots. Those of the crew whom he thought needed the liberty most got it. That included Sean and Ilaloa. The Lorinyan girl hadn't been well lately. A little blue sky might help.

When he stood on the ground, Sean drew a lungful of Nerthusian air and smiled down at

Ilaloa. "Is this better, darling?"

"Yes." Her voice came faint under the clangor of the spaceport.

Sean shook his head, tasting bitterness. "You'll get used to it," he said. "You couldn't expect to make a change like that all at once."

"I am happy," she insisted.

The memory of another face and another voice drifted through him. His mouth tightened and he walked from the port with long strides.

They left the concrete prairie of the spaceport behind them and strolled out on a wide avenue. It was a busy scene; humans and nonhumans hurrying on their way, cars and trucks filling the street with a steady roar, aircraft overhead. Ilaloa's hands went up to her ears. She smiled at him ruefully, but her eyes were darkened.

Even in that cosmopolitan crowd, they stood out. Sean wore Nomad costume—kilt, buskins, full shirt and tight jerkin, cape flowing behind him and bonnet slanted across his forehead. Ilaloa, in spite of her professed dislike for clothes, had adopted a loose filmy version of woman's dress. Against its dark blues and reds, the pale beauty of her was spectacular. Both wore side-arms, as crewfolk generally did on any planet except Rendezvous.

"Sean, Sean, let me go."

He drew Ilaloa aside, into a doorway. Her fingers plucked at his sleeve and the eyes turned to his were an unseeing blankness.

"Let me go alone for a little, Sean. It is only for the littlest time, away in the voice of trees. Oh, Sean, I want the sun!"

He stood for a moment, unsure, half-frightened. Then the simple realization came: Ilaloa couldn't take the city. She needed quiet.

"Why—sure," he said. "Of course. We'll go—"

"No, Sean, alone. I want to—think? I will come back."

"Well—well, certainly, if that's what you want." He smiled but his lips felt stiff. "Come on, then."

He guided her to a public aircar station, gave one of the vehicles some of his scanty Union credit notes, and told Ilaloa how to direct it. She wouldn't have far to go to reach a completely untenanted area, and they would meet again at the station.

She kissed him, laughing aloud, and slipped into the car.

Woods colt, he thought. He didn't dare consider if it would go with Ilaloa as it had gone with his settler wife.

I'm going to get drunk, he thought.

He walked swiftly until he was in the old section of town. Nobody stood on the law in that place. The native quarter was there, a result less of discrimination than of choice. The natives were friendly enough, but didn't feel comfortable in a human district. Tall bipedal beings, green-furred and four-armed, watched Sean out of expressionless golden eyes as he strode under trees and through barriers of flowering vines. Machines were not in evidence, except for a wooden cart drawn by one of the six-legged "ponies" of Nerthus.

The Comet Bar stood on the edge of the quarter, a small low-ceilinged structure where grass and pavement met. Sean walked in. A couple of colonists were drinking beer at a corner table; otherwise the place was deserted. Sean dialed for whiskey surrogate at the bar and sat down. He didn't want silence.

The door opened for a newcomer, admitting a brief sunbeam into the twilight of the room. Sean looked idly at the man. The fact of his being from Sol was plain from his dress: knee breeches and hose, loose tunic, light shoes, featherweight mantle with hood, all in subdued blues and grays. But it was the easy strength of him that stood out most.

He caught Sean's gaze and, after getting a drink from the dispenser, walked over and sat down beside the Nomad. "Hello," he said. The accent was unmistakable. "Don't see many of you fellows around."

"We come in now and then," grunted Sean.

"I've been in Stellamont for a couple of weeks," said the stranger. "Business, of sorts. But it's all wound up and I feel like celebrating. I wonder if you could recommend some good uninhabited places?"

"What business would a Solman have out here?" asked Sean.

"Research," said the Terrestrial. "Yes, you might call it that." He chuckled to himself and held out a pack of cigarettes. "Smoke?"

"Ummm—thanks." Sean took one and inhaled fire into it. Tobacco was expensive on the frontier; only the Earth-grown plant seemed to have the right flavor.

Sean wondered if it was true what they said about the exaggerated Solarian notions of privacy, and decided to find out. "What's your name?" he asked. "Can't just call you Solman."

"Oh, you can if you insist, but the name is Trevelyan Micah. And yours?" His black eyebrows lifted courteously.

"This one is called Peregrine Thorkild Sean. You could read the first two off my outfit if you knew the symbols. Also rank, ensign; and service, flier pilot and gunner."

"I didn't know you Nomads were organized so formally."

"It doesn't mean anything except in a fight." Sean drained his glass, tossed it down the nearest chute, and dialed for another. Trevelyan was still scarcely started on his. "Say we hit hostile natives, or an otherling ship that doesn't like us. That's where the ranks get important."

"I see. Interesting. Ordinarily, though, you're traders?"

"We're anything, friend. We can't make all we use or want—at least it isn't our way—so we float around, buy something cheap here, swap it for something else there, and finally sell what we have for Union credits. Or we might work a mine or something for a while ourselves, though usually we get the natives thereabouts to do it for us."

Trevelyan smiled. "Allow me." He bought the Nomad another drink. "Do go on. I've often wondered why your people choose to lead such a hard and rootless life."

"Why? Because we're Nomads. That's enough."

"Mmmmm-hm." Trevelyan grinned. "That reminds me of one time in the Sirian system—" He told an anecdote, and they started trading stories. Trevelyan drank in moderation; even so, his tongue began slipping a little.

"How about some solid fuel for a change?" he suggested at last.

"You're in your right orbit now," said Sean, speaking with elaborate precision. "But let's go where there's some life."

"Just as you say," responded Trevelyan amiably.

They had dinner in a small and noisy tavern which was beginning to fill up as the sun declined. Trevelyan kept making clumsy passes at the owner, a pneumatic human female. There was almost a fight, and they were frigidly escorted to the door.

"You're a good sort," said Sean, laughing. "A proper fellow, Micah."

"Electron shells," said Trevelyan owlishly. "We're only a pair of little electrons, jumping from shell to shell."

They went down the street, stopping in most of the bars that lined it. They were in a dim and smoky underground room when Trevelyan put his head on his arms, giggled stupidly, and went limp. Sean sat for a moment, blinking across the table at the man, wondering what to do.

"That will be four credits sixty," said a voice from high above. Sean saw a bearded giant with an uncompromising look about him. "That's your score, 'less you want something else."

"Uh—no." Sean felt in his pouch. Empty.

"Four credits sixty," said the giant.

"'M' frien's got it." Sean shook the unstirring Solarian. The shoulder was hard under his fingers, but the dark head rolled lax on the folded arms. Sean looked at the blurred form of the denkeeper, considered, and reached the triumphant answer.

He leaned over the table and groped in the Solarian's hip pocket until the leatheroid was in his hand. It was hard to focus. He opened the wallet and looked closer.

The luminescent words on the card within blazed at him:

TREVELYAN MICAH

FIELD AGENT A-1392-ZX-843

STELLAR UNION COORDINATION SERVICE

UNATTACHED

And the ringed star that burned over the letters, burned with its own cold fire and seemed to be spinning in dark space—

A Cordy!

Slowly, fighting himself every millimeter of the way, Sean paid the bill and slid the wallet back where it belonged. He couldn't think straight; he had to get a soberpill fast. This might not mean anything, but . . .

"Trevelyan! Trevelyan Micah!" Sean said.

"This is the district chief. Whassyer mission on Nerthus? Wake up, Trevelyan! Whassyer mission?"

"Nomads," mumbled the voice. "Catch a Nomad ship, chief. Lemme sleep."

CHAPTER VII

HIS HEAD ACHED a little in the smoke and noise of the inn, and Trevelyan had to resist the temptation to steal a glance and see what was happening about him. The landlord had been bribed carefully, and had played his part well.

He could almost feel Sean's eyes on him. The Nomad had bought a soberpill and spent a frantic quarter hour in a communication booth. Now he was sitting with one hand on his gun butt, staring and staring.

The affair had gone off like a robot gun so far.

Recognizing the early symptoms of worry, Trevelyan let his thoughts float free. Civilization was most complex and delicately balanced, but culture was not a physical thing—it was a process. Civilization was not material technology but a thought-pattern and an understanding. Then a voice broke into his thoughts.

"All right, Sean, what'd you get me out of bed for? I warn you, lad, it had better be good."

The voice was a strong resonant bass, speaking with an easy drawl, and the footsteps were heavy. Trevelyan's muscles wanted to leap.

"A C-Cordy, Hal. He's a Cordy. We g-got to drinking together and when he passed out, his wallet—" Trevelyan heard the young Nomad get up and strain across the table. "Here, see for y'self."

"Hm. Since when did Cordys carry this sort of thing? Or get sotted on the job?"

The newcomer was shrewd, thought Trevelyan. Actually his trick had been rather childish. He listened to Sean falter through an account of the evening.

"Ah, so. This one reckons you've been picked up, lad. Now let's see why." A calloused fist grabbed Trevelyan's hair and pulled his face up for inspection. "On purpose, too. This man's no more drunk than I am. All right, friend, you can quit now."

Trevelyan opened his eyes. For a satirical instant he enjoyed Sean's dumbfounded expression, then looked at the other man. This was a stout middle-aged fellow, his hairy body bare except for cloak, shoes, and gun belt—he must have been roused from sleep and come at once.

Trevelyan stretched luxuriously and sat back in the booth. "Thanks," he said. "I was getting somewhat tired waiting."

"You're a Solman, all right," said the Nomad, "and it wouldn't surprise me a bit to learn you really are a Cordy. Want to talk about it?"

Trevelyan hesitated a moment. "No. I'm sorry

you were awakened. Suppose I buy a round of drinks and we call it even.''

"You can buy the drinks," said the Nomad, plumping his large bottom onto the seat. "I'm not so sure about the rest of it, though."

Trevelyan signaled the proprietor. "There's been no real harm done," he insisted. "I'm not after you people, if that's what's worrying you. This was a—let's say an experiment."

"I'll need to know more than that."

"If you insist, I'll explain everything. But you wouldn't know whether it's the truth or not, so why bother?"

"There is that," said the Nomad. His face had gone expressionless.

The bearded man took their orders. They sat in silence, waiting.

Sean's voice exploded the quiet. "What to do, Hal?" He pushed the words out of a tautened throat. "What's going on?"

"We'll see." The reply was as wooden as the countenance.

"I'm—" Sean gulped. His face was drawn tight and there was a twitch in the angle of his jaw. "I'm sorry about this, Hal."

"All right, lad. If it hadn't been you, it'd have been somebody else. You at least had the sense to call me." The Nomad's eyes were cold on Trevelyan's, and when he smiled it was catlike. "Just to show we have some manners, I'm Peregrine Joachim Henry—rank, skipper."

Trevelyan nodded. "Hello," he said politely. "I want to warn you, Captain Joachim, against doing

49

anything rash.'' The phrase was carefully chosen on his guess about the other man's character. The melodramatic flavor should both irritate him and make him underestimate his opponent—very slightly, to be sure, but those things added up.

"I assure you," Trevelyan went on, "that you've nothing to fear." He smiled. "You seem to know that Coordinators don't run around with identification cards, like a fictional hero. So—how do you even know I am one? I could be a practical joker."

"It doesn't smell right, somehow," said Joachim bleakly.

The drinks arrived. They touched glasses and Joachim downed his in three gulps. Decision settled his features into an iron mold. "All right," he said. "You're coming along with us, lad, and at the first wriggle or squeak you get it. Sean will take you up to the *Peregrine*." He turned to the younger Nomad. "I've made all arrangements. The stuff'll be loaded tomorrow and we can leave at about eighteen hundred hours. If this person has friends looking for him, it isn't likely they'll think of us before we get clear of the system."

"Now wait a minute—" began Trevelyan.

"That'll do. We need to find out more about you, and there'll be a nice long voyage to do it in. If you keep clean, you won't get hurt, and we'll let you go eventually."

Trevelyan narrowed his eyes. "I won't say anything about charges of kidnapping," he murmured, "but how do you know I don't *want* to be taken aboard your ship?"

Joachim's grin flashed out, suddenly merry.

"Why, 'twouldn't surprise me at all if you did," he answered. "In which case, I wish you joy of it. All right, friends, let's drink up and get out of here."

Trevelyan walked meekly between the two Nomads. He didn't think of the many days of preparation—research in the Coordination and police files at Stellamont, tediously worked-out equations indicating psychological probabilities, study of the town, and rehearsal of his role. Those were behind him now, and for what followed he had no data, no predictions—

When they came to the spaceport—it must have been a good half-hour's walk and not a word spoken—the gate scanned them and opened. They crossed blank concrete, passing under the dim forms of slumbering spaceships, until they came to a hangar. The door there recognized its lessee and admitted them. There were a couple of small fliers resting here, and Sean opened the airlock of one. Lights came on within the ascetic interior, spilling out into the gloom of the building. Trevelyan saw that the fliers had a heavy retractable rifle in the nose and machine guns and missile tubes in the air fins.

Earth thought it had achieved peace, said his mind grayly, *and now this has bloomed again between the stars.*

He entered and sat obediently down in a recoil chair. Joachim lashed him fast with a few turns of wire. "I'll be going back to my lodgings," he said, yawning. "See that our boy is put under guard at the ship, Sean. Then you can come back here if you want to."

He went out and the airlock sighed shut behind

him. Sean's hands moved over the control panel with the deft ease of a skilled pilot. There was a mutter of engines and the panel flashed a clearance from the spaceport robot monitor. The landing cradle moved out of the hangar until it was under open sky. Sean smiled and touched the controls.

Trevelyan relaxed against the thrust of acceleration and looked ahead, out through the forward viewports. In minutes the atmosphere was below them and they were in space.

Trevelyan had seen that vision more times than he could remember, and yet each time it blazed for him with the same cold and undying magnificence. The darkness was like crystal, clear infinite black reaching beyond imagination; and against it, the stars were a bitterly brilliant radiance, white and aflame across the limitless night. *"The heavens declare the glory of God,"* he whispered, *"and the firmament showeth His handiwork."*

Sean gave him a puzzled glance. "What's that?"

"An old Terrestrial book," said Trevelyan. "Very old."

Sean shrugged and punched the computer keys. The flier mumbled to itself and swung about toward the *Peregrine's* calculated position.

The Nomad ship hove into view and Trevelyan studied her. She was a big cylindroid, two hundred and forty meters long from the blunt nose to the gravitic focusing cones at the stern, forty meters in diameter. There were three rings of six boathouses each around her circumference, holding spaceboats as well as fliers, and mounting a gun turret on top. Between each pair of boathouses was, alternately, a heavier rifle turret and a missile tube; and between the rings were the wide airlock doors of cargo-loading shafts. The vessel's flanks gleamed with a dull metallic luster; and as he neared, Trevelyan saw that the hide was worn, patched, pitted and seared in spots.

Sean landed expertly beside one of the boat-houses, clamping on, and a tube snaked from its small airlock to fasten over the flier's. Trevelyan felt a normal Earth weight pressing him from the hull.

"All right." Sean freed the prisoner. "Come along."

A bored-looking Nomad on guard duty straightened when he saw the new arrival. "Who is that, Sean?"

"Snooper." Sean's tone was curt. "Hal says to brig him."

The guard thumbed an intercom button and called for help. Trevelyan leaned against the metal wall and folded his arms. "It isn't necessary," he grinned. "I'm not going to make a fight."

"Say—" The guard's eyes grew wider. "You ain't a *Solman?*"

"Yes, of course. What of it?"

"Oh—just never seen a Solman before, that's all. I hope they don't finish you before I get a chance to ask about some things."

Several others arrived with sidearms in hand. They were a rather ordinary-looking bunch, if you excepted the earrings and tattoos of some. Trevelyan made absent, noncommittal replies to their questions and remarks, and was escorted off to his jail.

Under—gravitationally speaking, above—the

ship's skin, there was a five-meter space running almost the whole length of the cylindroid. On inquiry, Trevelyan learned that it contained public facilities and enterprises: the food plant and workshops, the recreational and assembly areas. A companionway took the party directly through this ring into the next concentric section, which had a three-meter clearance and was devoted to the residential apartments. The remainder of the ship was given over to control equipment and the great holds for supplies and cargo. Trevelyan was conducted down a hallway in the residential level.

He looked about him with an interested glance. The corridors, which intersected at frequent intervals, were about three meters wide, and lined with the doors of apartments. Underfoot the floor was carpeted with a soft springy material, dark green, most likely the produce of some world unknown to the Union. The walls were elaborately decorated with murals, or with panels of carved wood and plastic. Most of the doors were also wood or molded plastic, with ornamentation of hammered metal. Outside many apartments there were narrow boxes of soil, bearing flowers such as Earth had never seen.

His group accumulated quite a procession of Nomads, men and women and children; many looked highly intelligent. His bemused vision sharpened to sudden focus as one woman stepped from a doorway ahead of him.

She was young, and bigger than most, and there was grace in her movements. The hair that fell past the wide shoulders was a deep-blonde rush of waves, and the blue eyes were frank.

"Hello, who've you got there?" she asked. "Since when are we adopting Solmen?"

A couple of the guards scowled, and Trevelyan remembered that in Nomad society women had well-defined rights, but were expected to keep in the background. One of the younger men, however, smiled at her. "You ask him, Nicki. Sean brought him up but wouldn't say why, and neither will he."

"Who are you Solman?" inquired the woman, falling into step beside him. He noticed that her hands were smeared with clay, and that she held a shaping tool in one. "Sean's my brother-in-law, you know."

The archaic term reminded him that the Nomads had pretty clear-cut sexual mores—within the ship, at least. He smiled and gave his name. "Your captain has the idea I'm a Coordinator." He added, "So I was brought up here for— investigation."

Her look was slow. "You don't seem very disturbed by it."

Trevelyan shrugged. "What can I do?"

"You're being very cool. I think you *are* a Cordy."

The guards' faces stiffened and gun barrels lifted a trifle.

"Suppose I am?" he challenged.

"I don't know. It's up to Hal. But we don't torture, if that's any comfort to you."

"It is. Though I'd gathered as much from other sources."

The blue eyes were very steady now. "I wondered if you didn't want to be captured."

She was intelligent, maybe too much so. But she was eager to talk, and he might pick up some useful information. "Why don't you come see me at the brig?" he invited. "I'm guaranteed harmless."

"So is a gun until you squeeze the trigger. Sure, I'll come around. You won't be kept there long anyway, I think. After Hal's had a chance to question you, you'll probably be jettisoned or—" She stopped.

"Or killed?" Trevelyan gently.

She didn't answer, but that in itself was answer enough.

CHAPTER VIII

THE PEREGRINE slid from Nerthus and its star until she was in a sufficiently weak gravitational field, then the alarm bells warned crewmen to their posts. The indescribable twisting sensation of hyperdrive fields building up went through human bodies and faded, and the steady thrum of energy pulses filled the ship. Her pseudo-velocity grew rapidly toward maximum, and Carsten's Star dwindled in the rear-view screens and was lost among the constellations.

From astronaut to engineer, and all jobs between, the crew settled into a habitual round of ship duties. There was a relative dearth of automatic and robot machinery on a Nomad vessel, much being done by hand that a Solarian craft would have carried out for herself. This could in part be attributed to the decline of science among the star-jumpers. But there was also a genuine need for something to do when a large group of people, whose most fundamental motivation was an inbred restlessness, were crowded into a metal cylinder for weeks or months on end.

Off ship duty, the Nomads had enough occupation. Workshops hummed around the clock as artists and artisans produced goods to trade with their fellows or with outsiders. There were the children to take care of and educate, a serious task. There were the various entertainment and service enterprises, including three taverns and a hospital.

When Joachim thought the ship was properly under way, Trevelyan was escorted to the captain's cabin. Joachim dismissed the guard and smiled cheerfully, waving to a chair on the opposite side of his desk. "If you want a smoke, I have plenty of extra pipes."

"So you do." Trevelyan's gaze went about the room. It was laid out with a bachelor fussiness and a spaceman's compactness—in this corner the desk and a rack of astrogational instruments and references; in that corner a bunk and dresser. Doors led off to the tiny kitchenette and bathroom and to an extra bedchamber. A shelf of microbooks held an astonishing variety of titles in several languages, all seeming well used. There was a family portrait on the wall; against another wall was the customary family altar. A large rack held an unusually good collection of pipes, many of them intricately carved.

"They're mostly Nomad work. I made some of them myself," said Joachim. "But here's a curiosity." He got up and took a long-stemmed hookah from the rack. "A Narraconan death pipe. Enemies smoke it together—notice, it has two mouthpieces?—before a duel."

"Are you inviting me to have a puff?" asked Trevelyan blandly.

"Well, now, that depends." Joachim sat down on the edge of his desk, swinging one leg. "Would you answer some questions?"

"Of course."

Joachim went over to a closet and took out a small instrument. Trevelyan stiffened; he hadn't thought Nomads would have lie detectors.

"I got this one at Spica some years ago," said Joachim. "Comes in handy now and then. You don't mind?"

"No—no, go right ahead." Trevelyan sat back, and took conscious control of his heartbeat, encephalic rhythms, and sweat secretion.

Joachim attached the electrodes to determine encephalic output and cardiac rate. The Damadhva lie detector depended on sensing the abnormal pulsations created by the strain of telling a falsehood; but it had to be adjusted for each subject. As he answered the harmless calibrating questions, Trevelyan's nervous system maintained itself at an artificially high level, a camouflage.

"All right, lad, let's get to business." Joachim relit his pipe and looked up at Trevelyan through tangled brows. "You're a Cordy?"

"Yes, I am. And I did pick Sean up and get myself brought aboard your ship on purpose."

Joachim grinned. "You just pushed the buttons and we danced for you like robot dolls. Well, why?"

"Because it seemed the best way to contact you. If I'm correct, Joachim, the *Peregrine* is acting on a basis of information badly needed by the Stellar Union. I want to go along on your voyage."

"Mmmmmm-hm. And just what do you know?"

Trevelyan detailed what the integrators on Earth had gathered. "I'm pretty sure that there's another civilization in the Great Cross region," he went on, "that it knows of us, and that it is either actively hostile to us or damned suspicious. Why, I have no idea, but you can see that the Coordinators have to take immediate action. I decided that my best chance lay in joining forces with you. But you Nomads are all so wary of civilization that I had to manipulate things to get myself abroad."

"Ummm—yes, all right. Only how'd you know you'd be picked up by the one and only Nomad ship which is going to investigate this business?"

"I didn't, for sure. But it seemed reasonable that it would be the *Peregrine*—after all, it was her captain who was doing research in Stellamont."

"I see. And now what?"

"Now I want to go along with you and learn what you learn. There'll be other Coordinators working on this problem, of course, but I think my approach is the fastest. And it's urgent, Joachim!"

The Nomad rubbed his chin. "All right, you're aboard. I suppose you'll help us out, and I admit a trained Cordy could be mighty useful at times. Only suppose we break some Union laws, as could happen?"

"If it's not too serious, I won't bother about it."

"And suppose, if and when we come back, our decision on the matter is one you won't like?"

Trevelyan shrugged. "We can argue that out later."

"So we can. What else have you in mind?"

Up to then, Trevelyan had been truthful enough, as far as he went. Now, when he said, "Nothing in particular, except to make a full report to the integrators," it wasn't stretching verity too far.

Joachim asked a few more questions, then unclipped the electrodes and sat back with his feet on the desk and his hands clasped behind his neck. "Fair enough," he said. "All right, consider yourself the guest of the ship. Now, shall we pool what we know?"

The picture grew as they talked it out. Trevelyan had been aware of the old Tiunran voyages, but not of their or the Nomads' losses.

"I suspect that the aliens are colonizing the planets of G-type suns—or, at least, controlling them in some manner. They could easily scout around in our civilization. There are so many space-traveling species today that an intruder can easily pass himself off as a native of some Union planet. But their suspicion of us must be culturally based."

"How so?" asked Joachim.

"It's ridiculous on the face of it that they should want to conquer us for any economic gain, and they must know we have no such intentions toward them. Therefore, in spite of all good intentions, we probably represent a threat to them."

"How's that?"

"Our civilization may be so unlike theirs that contact would be devastating. Imagine, for example, that they have a very conservative aristocratic-religious setup. Interpretation by our culture would bring social upheavals their ruling class could not afford. That's only one guess, and most likely a wrong one.''

''I see.'' Joachim sat quiet for a while, puffing out smoke. Then: ''Well, we've a long trip ahead and lots of time to think.''

''Where are you going first?''

Joachim squinted. ''Erulan.''

Trevelyan searched his memory. ''Never heard of it.''

''You wouldn't have, and you'll stay aboard ship while we're there.''

''Reason?''

''It's illegal,'' said Joachim tightly. ''Let's think about you. You'll get along fairly well, if you aren't too obtrusive. But I'd suggest you get some shipboard garments. Less conspicuous.''

''How'll I do it?'' Trevelyan didn't push the question of Erulan.

''Well—'' Joachim reached in his desk drawer, pulled out a billfold, and tossed it to the other man. ''Here's your wallet back. Nice fat chuck o' money there. I picked up some clothes that're about your size. Couple of coveralls, shorts, boots, and so on. Sell you the lot for twenty credits.''

''*Twenty credits!* They'll be worth five at the most.''

''Well, I could let you have 'em for what they cost me. Fifteen.''

''If they cost you seven, I'll eat them—''

They haggled for a while, and finally settled for twelve credits—about one hundred percent profit.

Thereafter Joachim offered the Coordinator the extra bedroom at an only mildly exorbitant rental—along with meals prepared by his housekeeper, for an extra consideration. Trevelyan changed into shorts while Joachim happily counted his take.

"You might as well mooch around and get to know the ship," said the captain. He grinned. "Nicki's place is number two seventy-four."

"Do you know *everything* that goes on?"

"Just about." Joachim chuckled. "Nicki's a good sort, but not like the gossips say, so I wouldn't advise making passes at her."

Trevelyan went down the corridors at an easy pace, hands in pockets and dark face turning from side to side. Nomads stared curiously at him but none did more than nod a greeting. Apparently they were satisfied if their captain was. Trevelyan moved between the muraled walls and the carved doors and wainscots until he found the place he was looking for. No. 274.

The door stood ajar, between two posts graven in the shape of vine-covered trees. Sean's voice floated out: "Come in, Cordy."

Trevelyan entered. There was a bedroom on either side of the door; at the farther side the kitchen and bedroom flanked the exit to the other hall, so that the main body of the apartment was cruciform. One arm of the cross was given over to microbooks, music, tapes, and some rather good murals; the other was a cluttered workshop. Sean sat polishing his spacesuit, and beside him, sitting at his feet, was the Lorinyan girl whom Nicki had mentioned. She was, in truth, the most beautiful creature he had ever seen. Nicki was bent over a table, shaping a clay vase. She looked up and smiled. "You were right, 'Lo," she said.

"She's always right," said Sean. "She knows such things."

"What did she know this time?" asked Trevelyan. Sean was in a good humor apparently bearing no grudge, and Nicki was as friendly as before. Ilaloa—he wasn't sure.

"That you were coming," said Sean. "She senses you. Right, 'Lo?" His hand ruffled the fine silvery hair.

"A telepath?" Trevelyan. He kept his manner casual, but under it his mind was suddenly taut.

She spoke in the voice that was like singing, so low he could barely hear it: "Oh, I cannot—it is not of me to flow the words from the bound-in-darkness self. You are too lonely, all of you locked from each other and from knowingness. Some wills I can tell—the sly little animal-thoughts. But you of humanity, no."

"Then what—oh. Of course." Trevelyan nodded. "You can sense emissions, and each of us has a characteristic pattern."

"Yes, so." She was grave about it. Her look had become troubled now. "And yours is more—other—from mine than the Nomads'. You live more in your head than in your body, and yet it is not an inward sorrow to you, as it is to the men of Stellamont, who do not know what they are. You know, and have accepted it, and are strong in it—but never have I sensed such aloneness as is yours."

She lapsed into silence, as if frightened by her own words, and huddled close to Sean. Trevelyan regarded her for a long moment, not without pleasure. He saw a little shiver go under the lucent skin; there was a deep fright and grief in her, too, and she clutched Sean's knee.

Well, he thought, it's her problem. And Sean's, I suppose. She's too pretty for my taste.

He walked over to Nicki, answering her questions about his present status and intentions. The vase taking shape had the form of two battling dragons. "Nice," he said. "What'll you do with it?"

"Cast it in bronze and sell or swap it," she replied, not looking up. There was an earthiness about her which was at Galaxy's end from Ilaloa, he thought.

"Glad to have you along," she continued. "Maybe. What're your immediate plans?"

"Just to get acquainted and do some thinking. You know, I've been studying the Nomad art, and I'm convinced it's a new idiom. I daresay your literature is unlike ours too."

"We haven't got much, except for the ballads," she said.

"That's enough. Look how different American folk music was from the European—" She glanced at him in some puzzlement, then nodded. "I'd like to hear some when I get the chance."

"Well, I'll give you one right now," said Sean, putting away his spacesuit. He unslung a lorne from the wall and thrummed his fingers across the strings. His voice lifted in a ballad, the immemorial

65

theme of the faithless beloved . . .

> *"–She said to me, 'O Nomad, see*
> *I cannot follow you.*
> *The star ways were cold and dree*
> *where all the wild winds blew,*
>
> *the winds between the stars, my love*
> *the restless wander-call,*
> *blew low, blew high, into the sky,*
> *the withered leaves of fall,*
>
> *and we were blown, and all alone*
> *we flew from sunlit day*
> *into the waste where stars are sown*
> *and planets have their way–' "*

Sean grimaced. "I shouldn't have picked that one."

"Some other time," said Nicki. She turned to the Solarian, a little too quickly. "I didn't know you concerned yourself with things like that."

"In my work," answered Trevelyan, "everything is significant, and the arts are often the most highly developed symbolic form of a culture—therefore the key to understanding it."

"Are you always thinking of your work?" she asked, bridling.

"Oh, not always," he smiled. "One has to eat and sleep occasionally."

"I'll bet that trained mind of yours never stops," she said.

He didn't answer. In a sense, it was true.

Ilaloa stood up in one rippling movement. "If

you will forgive me," she said, "I think I will go to the park."

"I'll come along," said Sean. "Tired of sitting in here. Want to come, you two? We could have a beer down there."

"Not just yet," said Nicki. "I want to finish this vase."

"Then I'll keep you company, if I may," said Trevelyan.

Sean looked as relieved as courtesy allowed. He and Ilaloa went out, hand in hand. Trevelyan draped himself in a chair. "I don't wish to give offense, Nicki," he said. "Just tell me when I'm overstepping your mores."

"You weren't doing anything wrong. That ballad got Sean and Ilaloa to thinking, that's all." Briefly, Nicki explained the details.

"I see," he nodded. "It may not be good. Quite apart from social pressure, there's the fact that they can't have children, and in a family-based society like yours that'll come to mean a good deal in time."

"Well, I don't want to interfere," said the girl. Her voice was troubled. "Sean's always disliked children anyway. And he needs something now to take his mind off that other wench. Ilaloa—I don't know. She's not happy on board here, but she's shaking down as we travel. A niçe kid, I think— shy but nice."

"It's their lives," he agreed, shrugging.

She gave him a long look. "You know, Ilaloa wasn't so far off about you. You're too damned—what's the word?—Olympian."

"Solar civilization is based on the individual as a

unit, not the family or clan or state or anything else," he said. "Our psychodevelopment produces a certain attitude which—never mind, it's not important now. I'm not typical, anyway."

She thrust the work aside and ran a hand through her tangled hair. "You have it all figured out, haven't you?" she asked resentfully. "You know how the hidden machinery in you runs and how to push the right buttons in yourself—yes, I can see where you'd get to be lonefarers, all of you, and the Cordys more than everyone."

"Any individualist is isolated," he said, "but in our society he's not at odds with others, or with himself. Solitude comes natural."

She winced. "You've got me charted already, haven't you?"

"Not at all. Nor would I want to if I could."

"Let's have some music," she said, and strode across the room to the tapes. His vision followed her and ran along titles. There was a lot of old Terrestrial music.

Nicki took one out. "You know the *1812 Overture?*"

"Of course," he replied.

The first strains drifted through the room, loneliness and immensity of the winter steppe. Nicki returned to her work, gripping the clay with tight-sinewed force. "Tell me about Earth. "What's it like?"

"That's a contract job," he smiled. Within him, his mind wondered what to say. Could he tell her that Earth was less a planet and a population than it was a dream?

"We're not utopian," he said cautiously. "We have our troubles, even if they aren't the same as yours."

"What do you *do?*" she asked. Stepping back, she looked at the tentative molding of a dragon head, cursed, and wrenched it back into shapelessness. "What do you really want out of life?"

"Life itself," he told her. "And that isn't a paradox. Experience, understanding, adjustment and harmony—but struggle, too, making physical reality over toward a pattern."

He went on, keeping away from abstractions, speaking mostly of the little details of everyday life, of people and events and the land that held them. After a while, Nicki forgot her work and leaned over the table to listen, almost unspeaking.

CHAPTER IX

AT FULL cruising speed, it was about three weeks to Erulan. The time was put to good use by Joachim, who had to inform his crew that this was no ordinary voyage of discovery, trade, or exploitation. He let guided rumors circulate until it was common knowledge that the *Peregrine* was committed to scouting out a foreign and perhaps hostile domain. Playing down the dangers and building up the idea of possible huge profits—in addition to the amount already promised from the other Nomads—belonged in Joachim's devious tactics.

His public order came when they were close to their goal: because of delicate negotiations to be carried out, and the chance of assault from their hosts, there would be no liberty on the planet.

Trevelyan was a more difficult problem. Joachim spoke to the Coordinator early in the trip. "You won't like the truth," he declared, "but we'd better look the situation squarely in the face."

"I've been hearing some things about Erulan."

"Well, I'll begin at the beginning." Joachim stuffed his pipe with elaborate care. "About seventy-five years back, two new ships were founded, the *Hadji* and the *Mountain Man*. Only these were pretty ambitious young folks, who'd figured that regular Nomad life was too bare for them. Still, they couldn't see settling on some colony planet. Well, there was this barbaric world Erulan. With modern weapons, it wasn't hard to take over a warlike nation and help to conquer the rest. Now they sit on Erulan as bosses of a planet."

"Conquest." The word was bitter and obscene in Trevelyan's mouth.

"Oh, it's not so bad, now. They've only done to the natives what the natives were doing to each other. 'Course, all the other Nomads realized this could bring on real trouble with the Union, and passed laws against such capers, but by that time it was too late as far as Erulan goes. We still trade with the place, and they're one of the few cases where it was a Nomad ship that got diddled, instead of the other way around. But you can do pretty good business with 'em if you watch yourself."

Trevelyan's voice was blank: "What do you want with them now?"

"Information, lad. They're well into the Great Cross, and from little things I've picked up, I wonder if Erulan may not be in contact with X." Joachim veiled his face in smoke. "Cheer up, it's really not so awful."

"It's the sort of thing my service was set up to prevent."

"Which is why you're not going with us to the surface, nor are you going to get your hands on any astrogation instruments while we're in that neighborhood." Joachim grinned cheerily.

The ship was close to her destination when Joachim sent for Sean and Ilaloa. "Sean," said Joachim, "you're a good pilot, so I'm letting you take me down to the planet. And there's no reason why Ilaloa can't go."

The younger man inhaled a cigarette. "What's your real motive?"

"You don't rank high enough to be paid much attention to. You might as well take your lady on a stroll through town. Sight-seeing. And if that telepathy or whatever-it-is of hers should just happen to pick up some thoughts—oh, let's suppose thoughts about X aliens on Erulan, or even the thoughts *of* those otherlings—it'd be interesting, wouldn't it?"

"You could have said it in half the words," replied Sean. "All right, Captain, if Ilaloa's willing."

"This is my ship too," she answered.

On the twenty-third day from Nerthus, the *Peregrine* flashed out of hyperdrive and approached the sun of Erulan on gravity beams.

Joachim sat in the bridge, waiting for his communications man to raise the planet. The internal gravity field made the outer hull "down," so that the big vision screens were underfoot. The screen buzzed and hummed with cosmic interference, the wordless talking of the stars. There was silence on the bridge, only the patient voice of the operator spoke. "Nomad ship *Peregrine* calling Erulan Station. Come in, Erulan. Come in, Erulan.''

A streaked image grew on the screen.

The man that finally looked out was a hard-visaged sort, gorgeous in the furs and jewelry of a noble. His head was shaven, except for a queue, and he spoke with an accent. ''What do you want?''

Joachim went over to stand in front of the screen. ''Captain Peregrine speaking for his ship,'' he said easily. ''We're coming in toward your planet. Like to pay a call.''

''There is no trading just now.''

''We weren't going to trade. Only wanted to say salute, me and a few of my officers. All right if we take an orbit and send a boat down?''

''Visitors are not being received.''

''You got a new Arkulan?''

''No. Hadji Petroff is still in command. But—''

''Now look, lad,'' said Joachim, ''this one knows your king's sociable. Since when did he give *you* the right to turn down company for him?''

''I speak for His Majesty. And use proper respect, Peregrine!''

''To you?'' Joachim grinned nastily. ''I'm a peaceful man, but please remember the *Peregrine's* not unarmed. Any time we feel like turning our Long Johns on you, there's nothing you have to say about it. If the Arkulan doesn't want to see us, let him tell me so himself—but ask His Majesty to remember that I'd be most terribly disappointed if he said no. Now give me an orbit and jump to it!''

The proud face stiffened with anger. ''That could get you killed.''

''Before you try, lad,'' answered Joachim, ''you

73

might think a bit." His tones became a roar. "How long do I have to talk with underlings? If there's any reason for denying us planetfall, let the Arkulan tell me. Now get!" He snapped off the screen.

"Whee-ew!" First Mate Ferenczi's teeth gleamed white in his beard. "That's a long chance, Hal. If you got him really mad—"

"No," said Joachim, relaxing. "That one wouldn't be coming to the 'visor on call' if he were a big engine. He's used to bullying his underlings and being bullied by his masters. Since he doesn't know just where I fit in, his natural reaction is to crawl. He'll refer the matter higher up."

"But why should they object?" Ferenczi's gaunt face drew into a scowl. "Erulan's never been hostile to Nomads before."

"It was coming, Karl. They're being absorbed by their conquests. Eventually, they're going to shun all outside contact, because it'd upset their little wagon." Joachim puffed hard. "My guess is, there's something going on behind the Arkulan's back."

"We'd better signal battle stations."

"Yeah. And fliers up, detectors out, everything we've got. Still, I don't expect it'll come to a fight. They'll try to cover up."

A human of top rank was presently on the screen—Mountain Man Thorkild Edward, whom Joachim knew. With him, the Nomad captain was ingratiatingly genial, dropping broad hints of rich gifts, but there was a carefully expressed clash of iron in his voice. It ended with a left-handed apology for the behavior of the subordinate and an invitation for the whole crew to land. Since that would put them all at Erulanian mercy, Joachim pleaded a rush and accepted on behalf of himself and a few officers only.

The *Peregrine* took an orbit close to the planet, but instead of falling free remained directly above Kaukasu. It was an impolite but completely unambiguous gesture. Joachim left Ferenczi in command and chose younger men from astronautics and engineering to accompany him. They'd be a good, harmless-looking front. He winced as he selected presents for his hosts—a small fortune in ornamental objects.

A boat took the festive-clad party down. Sitting near Sean, Joachim saw the planet as a somber disc in the sky, storm-belted, its frigid oceans washing against steep-cragged mountains, the northern hemisphere bleached with snow-fields.

The city of Kaukasu lay in about twenty degrees north latitude, where agriculture was possible. It had been the seat of native warrior-kings, and the new masters hadn't changed it much—the palaces had been air-conditioned and a military base set up. Joachim saw new buildings on the edge of town, a small shipyard.

"That's a funny one," he murmured. "I'd've sworn the humans here had about given up space travel. What use is it to them?"

The boat landed on the field before the central castle. This was on a terraced hill rising out of the middle of Kaukasu, each terrace ringed by heavy walls of age-blurred stone. Below it, the city sprawled in a chaos of high roofs and bulbous towers, out to the fields and the great forests. On the horizon a rim of mountains lifted white and ragged into the deep purplish heaven. There was traffic in the narrow streets, throngs of natives on foot, mounted, a rare groundcar pushing through turbulent crowds.

Joachim stepped from the airlock and wrapped his mantle around him, shivering. A guard of honor waited, ranked like statues. They lowered spears in salute as a fur-clad human approached.

The Erulani were quite manlike, and were stoutly built, their skins a deep amber-yellow, their faces rather flat and Mongoloid. There were only four fingers to a hand, the ears were large and pointed, the males completely bald. The eyes were the least human feature: under a single straight line of black brow, they were oblique and felinoid—all smoky-red iris, slit-purpled and unwinking. These, the soldiers, wore long blue tunics over legginged breeches and beryllium-copper chain mail, spiked helmets, curved swords at the right side.

Mountain Man Thorkild stopped a couple of meters from the Peregrines and bent his queued head as if it pained him. "Greeting and welcome," he said. The wind shrilled under his words and blew them across the barren flag-stones. "The Arkulan awaits you."

"Thanks," said Joachim. "Come along, boys."

His men trailed after him, carrying the boxes of gifts. Sean and Ilaloa stayed within the boat, partly to guard it and partly because Joachim didn't fancy what might happen if Hadji Petroff's eye fell on the girl. Rhythmic footfalls beat on stone as the guard tramped in the rear. A gorgeously dressed trumpeter blew a flourish when they came to the castle gates.

And I think the ships stand too much on ceremony! reflected Joachim.

But it was inevitable. The ex-Nomads had taken over a barbaric system; it followed with the ruthless logic of history that they would themselves be barbarized.

Every human male was a high noble, and every Erulani—in theory—a slave. Modern weapons were only permitted to the overlords; the natives remained in the early Iron Age. Tribute was exacted from a swollen empire to support the masters in luxury. On the surface, it looked as if the Hadjis and the Mountain Men had a good thing.

But, Joachim's thoughts continued, they were themselves captives of their own creation. The court seethed with intrigue and corruption. No strong man could rest; he must always be watching for betrayal from his savagely ambitious underlings or murder from his wary superiors. Human speech and dress and dreams were being lost, as one by one the victors took over the patterns of their slaves. A verse went through the Peregrine's memory. *What shall it profit a man if he gaineth the whole world and loseth his own soul?*

They went through looming vaulted halls until they reached the audience chamber. It was a monstrous place, the roof lost in a dusk of sheer height, the narrow windows throwing bloody lances of sunlight onto the thick-piled rugs. The room shouted with gold, jewels, banners and tapestries; the walls were lined with rigid native guards, and a swarm of slaves prostrated themselves before Kaukasu's enthroned nobles. Trumpets blew again above a thunder of kettledrums.

Joachim and his men kowtowed ceremonially before the Arkulan. This was a middle-aged man, stiff in his robes, the crowned head erect with arrogance. But he greeted them well—more hospitably than some of his barons, who gave the Nomads ugly glances. *Uh-huh. They've got business under way that the chief doesn't know about, and it involves their not wanting visitors.*

Chairs were brought for the guests. Joachim distributed his gifts and sat down, smoking and gossiping with the Arkulan. As wine was drunk, the company relaxed, and there was no difficulty about getting the king's permission for such crewmen as wished to go sight-seeing.

"But I'll try to entertain you here," said Petroff. "It's been a long time since we had a ship drop in. Why aren't you coming to trade?"

"We have other business, Your Majesty," said Joachim.

"Ah, so? Looking for new territories?"

"I wouldn't," said Thorkild. "By now, you should know the Great Cross doesn't have enough civilization to make exploration worth while."

"Oh, I don't know," responded Joachim. "What're you building those new ships for if not to do some starfaring for yourselves?"

"I'm having that done," said another noble, Hadji Kogama, "since I have the slaves and the machinery. But I only take them to Sara—you know the planet?"

"N-no. Too many planets for a man to remember."

"It's a long and not very interesting story," said Kogama, "but they're a backward system out Canopus way who've been visited a few times by Galactic Survey and would like a space fleet. An agent of mine was on Thunderhouse a few years back to make some purchases, and happened to meet one of theirs who was looking for a contractor to build them ships. I arranged to do it. The ships are flown to Sura and paid for in goods. Naturally, the natives don't know where their contractor lives, but they don't care, either."

"I see." *Like hell I do! Since when did an Erulani noble turn manufacturer—or bother explaining himself in such detail?*

"But what are you here after?" persisted Thorkild.

Joachim invented a planet. It had good trading possibilities, but the social structure was an elaborate master-slave system with an unbelievable ceremony-fetish. He wanted to get some pointers from Kaukasu as to how the natives should be handled.

"It's a long way to come just for information," said Petroff.

"Oh, not actually, Your Majesty," said Joachim. "We've found us a world not very far from here—satellite of a J-planet—with some pretty rich ore lodes. Since we were going there anyway, it wasn't much off our track to stop by Erulan."

"Where is this system?" asked Thorkild.

Joachim looked pained. "Now really," he said, "you don't expect me to tell you that, do you?"

Petroff chuckled. "No, I reckon not."

A banquet was given after sunset. When enough liquor had disappeared, the affair got as wild as a Nomad Mutiny. Joachim was sorry to miss it, but he thought it advisable to swallow a soberpill in advance and merely play drunk. His shipmates didn't act, but secrecy toward outsiders was a conditioned relfex in every proper crewman. He himself let slip a tantalizing hint or two in the right direction, and noticed Thorkild's eyes. The fish was nibbling.

When he finally steered a wavering course to his bedroom, he found that the Arkulan had hospitably provided him with a servant.

The girl didn't rank high in the harem, but she knew some gossip and Joachim bribed it out of her. It didn't *prove* that Thorkild and Kogama, among others, were conspiring against the Arkulan; but it was enough for his purposes.

He wandered about the castle the next day, asking questions that fitted his ostensible reason for being there, and wasn't surprised when a slave handed him a note requesting his attendance on Thorkild. He followed the native along a warren of corridors and up a ramp into one of the towers. There was a chamber just below the roof, its windows open to a frosty air and a dizzying downward view. The place was austerely furnished, more like an office than a noble's reception room. Thorkild sat behind a desk, his body wrapped in furs, his shaven head bent over some papers.

80

"Sit down, Peregrine," he invited curtly, not looking up.

Joachim found a chair, crossed his legs, and got out his pipe.

Finally the long, lean face turned to him. "Have you learned what you came here for?" asked the baron.

"Oh, I've gotten a few useful ideas," said Joachim.

"Let's not feint." Thorkild's countenance was immobile and unreadable. "This room is spy-proofed. We can talk plainly. What did you mean last night when you said the Great Cross had some very interesting possibilities? And when you said it was a pity Hadji Kogama was building ships for Sura, when a really juicy market lay right to hand?"

"Well," said Joachim, "I have a low mind. Things occur to me. Like the possibility that Kogama wasn't selling his ships at all, but just stockpiling them somewhere until he has enough of a fleet to take over this business."

"He isn't doing that. I know."

"Because you're both figuring to run Erulan?"

"We aren't traitors." Thorkild's voice was flat.

"Mmmmmm—no, I never said that. Only His Majesty might misinterpret certain information. Such as—" Joachim mentioned a suborned vizier and a captain of household troops to whom promises had been made.

"If you start meddling in things that are none of your concern," flashed Thorkild, "I might forget you're a guest."

"If you do, lad, you'll be the first fatality. And if I don't come back, the *Peregrine* will start bombarding." Then, with a smile: "But let's not fight, Ed. We're old friends, and I know this isn't my business. As a matter of fact, I wanted to pass the word to you."

"What word?"

"Palace scuttlebutt. Maybe it means something, maybe it doesn't."

"How could you learn secrets I can't get?"

"I'm a stranger. The women find me interesting—really, that purdah you keep 'em in must get awful boring. They know I'll be gone tomorrow, and meanwhile I give 'em some nice presents. Why shouldn't they talk to me? And why shouldn't they intrigue in the first place?"

Thorkild tugged nervously at his queue. Joachim could almost read the thoughts inside that narrow skull. There was no chance for a noble to torture secrets out of the royal concubines. "What have you learned?" he asked finally.

"Well—" Joachim looked at the ceiling. "I've always thought of you as my friend, Ed. I gave you some pretty good things yesterday."

They argued over the bribe till Joachim had recouped a fair percentage of his earlier outlay. Then he said, untruthfully—but it was based on a shrewd guess—"Kogama has harem and royal guard contacts you may not know about. Word circulates. There's a rumor that you and several others are associated with Kogama in building this fleet. Only the ships are staying right here."

Thorkild's face was utterly masklike. To

Joachim, that was as good an indication as any. He fed the noble a concoction of hints and whispers suggesting that Kogama had plans for his own allies, when their mutual scheme had gone through. *It might even be correct, at that!*

There was a silence when the narrative was finished. Thorkild sat resting his chin in one hand, the fingers of the other drumming on the desk top.

Joachim waited a moment, then leaned forward confidentially. "I'd like to make a guess, Ed." he murmured. "I think there's another civilization in this volume of space. I think they're hiding from man, Cosmos knows why. But you're building ships for them, you and your clique. The— strangers—are paying you well, I imagine in gold, so that you can build up an organization. The present Arkulan's a pretty smart boy. He's arranged things so it'd be hard to overthrow him, but you think you can do it with that new wealth. Am I right?"

"If you were, what would you do with the knowledge?"

"I don't know. It might be sort of interesting to meet those aliens. May be money in it. Or if they're hostile to us, the ships ought to know about it." His eyes lifted and held the other man's. "I'd like to ask you one thing, though, Ed. If a powerful otherling empire grows up all around Erulan, what good is the throne here to you?"

"They aren't otherlings, or natives." Thorkild's tones were strained. "They're human."

Human!

"They're a strange sort. Talk Basic with the

weirdest accent, don't wear clothes, don't—I don't know. They have the ways of natives, but they're human, I'll swear."

"What do they want?" asked the Peregrine.

"Ships. They contacted us about five years ago. Yes, they pay in metal, and I gather they're from somewhere in the Cross. But that's a very big region, Joachim. Maybe it's foolish of us to deal with them, but you don't get ahead except by taking chances."

"No," agreed Joachim. "No, you don't."

CHAPTER X

IT WAS NEAR evening of the first day that an Erulani brought a scribbled note from Joachim out to
the spaceboat. *"All right to go prowling in town,
but don't go too far. We may have to leave in a
hurry."* Sean stood for a moment in the airlock,
straining his eyes to read in the last dull light. The
wind was low and cold; beneath the castle, roofs
and towers were black against the sky.

Ilaloa sat up on one elbow as he entered the
bunkroom. "It's too late to go out now," he said.
"We'll do it tomorrow morning. Is that all right?"

She nodded.

"I know you don't like being penned here," he
said. "I'm sorry."

"It is nothing. I was gone in thoughts, Sean."

He stood regarding her. His eyes followed the
gentle curve of her body to the face, and rested.
"You wish you were back on Rendezvous, don't
you?"

85

She smiled, and then suddenly she laughed. It was like a tinkling of bells. "Poor silly Sean. You think too much." He drew her against him and she pressed close. His mouth brushed the fragrance of her hair and closed the parted lips below his.

Well—she's right. I worry too much, and it gets me nowhere.

Gently, he disengaged himself. "How about some solid fuel?"

She nodded and moved lightly to the boat's gravity shaft. "This falling up is fun," she called. "You have so many toys."

"Toys?" he echoed. But she was already gone, floating along the upward beam toward the galley near the bows.

The next morning, he donned Nomad folk dress but added a heavy tunic. He had to wait for Ilaloa to finish her shower. She was always taking long baths aboard ship, as if to wash off some hidden uncleanliness.

"Put on some thick clothes, dear," he advised, feeling a warm husband sense within him.

She wrinkled her nose. "Do I have to?"

"If you don't want to freeze out there, yes. What's wrong with dressing, anyway?"

"It is the—shut-away from sun and rain and all the many winds," she answered. "There is a dead skin around and it is another darkness. You are locked from life, Sean." But she did clothe herself and danced eagerly before him to the airlock.

The morning was chill and misted; wet flagstones gleamed underfoot as they went toward the outer gates. They walked under mountainous towers and down the hill into the city.

It was already awake, and its noise grew loud as they entered the streets—shrill clamor of voices, thump of hoofs, groaning wheels and clashing iron. The smells were there, too. Sean snorted and glanced down at Ilaloa. But she didn't seem to mind; she was looking around with a wide-eyed wonder he hadn't seen in her before.

The streets were narrow and cobbled, slippery with muck, twisting fantastically between the high walls of peak-roofed houses. Doors were heavy and brass-bound, windows no more than narrow slits; overhanging balconies shut out the sky. Flimsy wooden booths lined the façades, each with its wares on display—pottery, clothing, tools, weapons, rugs, food, wine, all the poor needs and luxuries of the planet cried by their raucous merchants. Here and there a temple stood, minareted and grotesquely ornamented with the blood-smeared effigies of gods.

The crowd swirled about Sean and Ilaloa, trying hard not to jostle the sacred human figures but sometimes pushed against them. It was the kind of spectacle which is only romantic at long range. Sean thought he could feel the violence that boiled around him.

Ilaloa tugged at his sleeve and he stooped to hear her under the din. "Do you know this city, Sean?"

"Not very well," he admitted. "I can show you a few sights if—" He hesitated. "If you want to."

"Oh yes!"

A trumpet brayed up ahead, and the Erulani sprang to the walls. Sean pulled Ilaloa with him, aware of what was coming. A squad of guardsmen galloped past, armored and helmeted, mud sheeting from the hoofs. Their bugler had a lash that he swung about him. There was a human in their midst, the chief, dressed even as they.

A woman screamed in the wake of the troop. Before the crowd had filled the street again, Sean saw that she was bent over a small furry shape. Her child had not been fast enough.

His throat was so tight that it hurt him. "This way, Ilaloa," he said. "Back this way."

"There was death," said Ilaloa quietly.

"Yes," he replied. "That's the way Erulan is."

They entered another thoroughfare. There was a procession of slaves coming, chained neck to neck. Their feet bled as they walked. A couple of soldiers urged them along with whips, but they didn't look up.

Sean regarded Ilaloa again. She stood watching the slaves go by, but somehow the compassion in her face didn't go deep.

A gallows was in the market square on which the street opened. Three bodies swung aloft. Beneath them, a gallantly clad Erulani was thrumming a small harp. It was a happy tune.

Ilaloa's fingers tightened around his. "You are with grief, Sean."

"It's this damned, bloody planet," he answered. "It's all so unnecessary!"

She looked steadily at him, and her voice was serious. "You have been long shut away from life," she said. "You have forgotten the sweetness of rain and summer nights. There is a hollowness in your breast, Sean."

"What has that got to do with this?"

"This is life around us," she said. "You have

forgotten how it can be hot and dark and cruel. You burn your dead in fire and forget that flesh molders into earth. The land should be strong with your bones and blossom where you died. You would have it forever day, not remembering night and storm. You live with ghosts and dreams in your own darkness. That is wrong, Sean.''

''But *this—!*''

''Oh, it is hard and angry here, but it lives in the now. Are you afraid of the riving and screaming in childbirth? Do you fear to remember the hunter by moonlight, how she strikes down life to feed her young? Do you know the lust of killing and ruling?''

''You d-don't think that's right, do you?''

''No. But it *is*. Oh, Sean, you cannot love life till you are life, all of it, not as it should be, but as it is, laughter and grief, cruelty and kindness, beyond yourself— No, you do not understand.''

They walked on. After a moment, she said gently, ''Oh, the real can be made better. There is no need for this endless strife and suffering. But it is still more—right—than that which is in the city Stellamont.''

''You mean,'' he asked, ''that reason is wrong? That instinct—''

She laughed, though it had a wistful tone. ''You are kind, but your kindness is so far away.'' Suddenly she almost cried aloud. ''Oh, Sean, if we could have children—''

He drew her close to him, forgetting the cat-stares around, and kissed her. Somehow, he felt lightened. They had tried to know each other, and even the failure was a kind of victory.

After lunch, the thoroughfares emptied as city folk retired for a siesta. They wandered into a labyrinth of crooked streets and blind alleys and were lost. That wasn't serious; they need only go in the general direction of the castle to spot it from some open plaza.

Sean peered up a street, a narrow tunnel under crazily leaning houses, wondering if it might lead somewhere. "Shall we try this?"

There was no reply. He hadn't expected it; Ilaloa left half his questions hanging. But when he turned around, he was shocked.

He had seen love in her face, merriment, alarm, grief, loneliness, disgust, timidity, and the blankness of withdrawal. But he had never before seen her really frightened.

"'Lo—what's wrong?" he whispered it, and his gun seemed to slide of itself from the holster.

Her eyes sought his, strickenly. One hand covered her opened mouth as if to fend off a shriek. *"Amuriho,"* she gasped. *"Hualalani amuriho."*

He drew her behind him, against the wall, and faced out into the street. It was empty.

"A thought. A thought from—no, Sean!"

He didn't look at her. His eyes hunted up and down the road where nothing stirred. "X," he said.

"It was not of man and not of Erulan," she breathed shakingly. "It was cruel and a hollow night filled with stars. And cold, cold!"

"Where?"

"Near this place. Behind some wall,"

"We're getting out of here!"

"Again—there it is again!" She clawed at his

body, thrusting close. Her face was buried against him and he felt her shiver.

"C-can you read the mind?" he stammered.

"Darkness," she gulped. "Darkness and emptiness, full of stars, a picture of stars like a sickle around a shining field."

The gun butt was slippery in his hand. "Can they sense us?"

"I do not know." The whisper was raw, there in the bloody twilight. "It thinks of stars beyond stars, but always that picture of a sickle reaping shiningness. There is scorn and mastery in it, like steel and—" Her voice trailed off.

"It is gone again now," she said in a small and childlike tone. "I cannot feel it any more."

He broke into a trot, holding her wrist with one hand and the gun with the other. "Joachim's hunch was right," he said between his teeth. "Now we've got to get off this planet!"

CHAPTER XI

NO ONE could accuse the ships of bearing a particularly intellectual society; still, reading was one way to pass the long times of voyage. The *Peregrine*, like her sisters, had a fair-sized library. It was a long double-tiered room in the outer ring, near the waist of the ship and not far off the park. Trevelyan had spent a good deal of time there on the journey from Nerthus.

He wandered in now. It was quiet, almost deserted save for the dozing attendant and a couple of old men reading at a table. The walls were lined with shelves holding micro-books from civilized planets: references, philosophies, poetry, fiction, *belles-lettres*, an incredible jackdaw's nest of anything and everything. But there were also large-sized folios, written by the natives of a hundred worlds or by the Nomads themselves. It was the compendious history of the ships which he took down and opened.

It began with the memoirs of Thorkild Erling, first captain of the Nomads. The bare facts were known to every educated person in the Union by now: how the first *Traveler*, an emigrant ship in the early days of interstellar voyaging, blundered into a trepidation vortex—then a totally unsuspected phenomenon, and even now little understood—and was thrown some two thousand light-years off her course. The hyperdrive engines of that day had needed a good ten years simply to get back into regions where the constellations looked halfway familiar; and after that, the vessel had ranged about for another decade, hopelessly searching. They found an untenanted E-planet, Harbor, and built their colony, and most of them were glad to forget that wild hunt through the deeps of forever. But a few couldn't; so in the end, they took the *Traveler* and went out once more.

That much was history. Now, reading Thorkild's words, Trevelyan caught something of the glamour which had been in those first years. But dreams change. By the very fact of realization, an ideal ceases to be such. There was a note of disappointment in Thorkild's later writings; his new society was evolving into something other than what he had imagined. *That's humanity again, never really able to follow out the logic of its own wishes.*

Trevelyan paged rapidly through the volume, looking for hints on the evolution of Nomad economy. A spaceship can be made a closed ecology, and the Nomad vessels did maintain their own food plants—hydroponics, yeast-bacteria synthesis of protein foods and vitamins—as well as doing a lot of their own repair, maintenance, and construction work. Cut adrift, they could last indefinitely. But it was easier and more rewarding to exploit the planets, as traders and entrepreneurs.

It was not all trade—sometimes they might work a mine or other industry for a while; and robbery, though frowned on, was not unknown. From whatever they gained, they took what was needed and used the rest for barter or sale.

Such enterprises were always carried out by individuals or groups of individuals, once the captain had made whatever preliminary arrangements were necessary. A small tax was enough to support the various public facilities and undertakings.

The society was democratic, though only adult men had the franchise. Matters of general Nomad policy were settled at rendezvous, the Captains' Council being empowered to make certain decisions while others were referred to the crews. Within a ship, the assembled men discussed and voted on whatever issues the captain couldn't handle as routine, and all the Nomads seemed quite passionately political-minded. The captain had broad powers and, if he used it right, an even broader influence—the fact that Joachim could take the *Peregrine* scouting this way, on his own decision, spoke for itself. If—

Trevelyan glanced up with a sudden consciousness and felt his pulse quicken. Nicki had just come in.

She had a book under one arm, which she replaced on its shelf. Turning, she smiled at him. "Where've you been the last few days? I've hardly seen you."

"Around," he said vaguely. "Anything new?"

She shook her head, and the light slid across its dark yellow tresses. "I'm weaving now," she told him. "Ferenczi Mei-Ling—Karl's wife, you know—wants a new rug, and she can pay for it." The broad forehead drew into a scowl. "Nothing new ever happens."

"I should think your whole Nomad life was founded on the idea of having something new always happening," he said.

"Oh, we jump from one planet to another still crazier, but what does it mean?"

"Life," he reproved with a smile, "has no extrinsic purpose or meaning; it's just another phenomenon of the physical universe, it simply *is*. And that's also true of any society. What you're angry about is that you can't find a purpose for yourself."

Her eyes were smoky-blue, meeting his. "There you go again!" she flared. "Can't you look at anything or do anything at all without it as a—a specific case of a general law?"

As a matter of fact, thought Trevelyan, *no*.

Aloud, he said mildly, "I have my fun. I like a glass of beer as well as the next man. Speaking of which, will you join me in a gulp?"

"You're not answering me," she accused him. "It's always the same. Women can't think! Leave them with the kitchen and the kids. I'm getting sick of it!"

"I'm a Solarian," he reminded her. "We'd be the last to have ideas of male superiority."

"Sol—" For an instant her expression softened, the long soot-black lashes dropped and she breathed the word with a caress. Then, scornfully:

"What has Sol to offer? What are you doing there but trying smugly to run the universe according to a bunch of—of equations? A theory!"

"Any culture is based on a theory," he said. "Ours simply happens to be explicitly formulated."

"There are times when I hate you," she said, and her fists clenched.

"I'm not trying to talk down to you," he snapped. "If I wanted to tell you a soothing fairy tale, you'd never know I was doing it. But don't spit on what you can't understand!"

She countered his gaze steadily and then, amazingly, smiled. "All right, I surrender," she laughed. "Let's go for that beer, shall we?"

And I thought I was a good psychologist! Trevelyan reflected wildly.

A siren whooped. Nicki stiffened, listening to the blasts.

"What's that?" he asked.

"Signal," she answered tightly. "Battle stations alert. All hands stand by for hyperdrive."

"This close to the planet?"

"It may be urgent." She ran over to the library Eye.

There were many such televisor screens aboard—each apartment had one, as well as public places. They would be tuned to any of the scanners throughout the ship, strategically mounted to give a view of all points where something of general interest might happen. Nicki dialed swiftly past scenes from the airlocks. The Nomad readers crouched by her and Trevelyan looked over their shoulders.

Minutes stumbled by before the flickering screen steadied on one image. Trevelyan recognized the egress from one of the boathouses. Joachim was just emerging, and his face was grim.

His words roared out of the ship's loudspeakers. "Attention, all Peregrines! This is the captain. We're getting out of here on gravity drive at once. You hear me, engine room? Full gravity drive north from the ecliptic at once. Stand by to go into hyper if necessary." The voice relaxed a little. "No, I don't *think* we're being chased or that they're angry with us on Erulan, but you can't tell. We've picked up some information that could be worth a lot of lives, and we're going where it's safe to know things."

Trevelyan felt the deck quiver, ever so faintly, with the forward surge. Gravitic acceleration being uniform on all objects, he experienced no pressure, but he imagined they were running skyward at a good fifty G's.

Joachim's voice jarred him. "Will Trevelyan Micah please report to me on the bridge at once? I'll need some help on this."

Nicki thrust past the men. "What can it be?"

"That's what I'm going to find out," said Trevelyan.

"Then I'll come, too."

Joachim stood by the astrogational computer, letting Ferenczi direct the ship. Sean was on hand, his thin features twisted. But it was to Ilaloa that Trevelyan's eyes went. She sat in the astrogator's chair, crouched over the desk, and he could see how tension bent her form into a bow.

"What's the matter?" he asked.

"I'm not sure yet—" Joachim looked at Nicki, who stood above Ilaloa with one hand laid on the Lorinyan's head. "What're you doing here?"

Nicki lifted her face and stamped one foot. "Any objections?"

"Well, no, I reckon not. Maybe you can calm down the girl. She's had a pretty bad fright." He relayed in curt words what had been learned on Erulan: humans of strange habits secretly buying spaceships, and Ilaloa's reception of a thought no mind should have had to endure. "They broke in on me, she and Sean, just when I was thinking of leaving," he finished. "That settled it. 'Lo's a good girl, though. She didn't break down till we were safe."

Trevelyan regarded the two women. Ilaloa was weeping on Nicki's breast now, sobs tearing at her.

"A really alien thought?" inquired the Terrestrial. "But if she can't read our minds, how could she read this?"

"Wave-patterns vary." Sean's answer was harsh. "This chanced to be one more like her own than man's is. But the content of it was—other."

"Micah, what do you make of this?" asked Joachim.

"Well—assuming it wasn't a mistake or something—hm." Trevelyan rubbed his chin. "Humans in the one case, aliens in the other. Could they be operating independently, maybe unaware of each other?"

"Well," said Joachim dubiously, "I reckon they could, but it just doesn't seem very believable."

"Maybe not. I have an idea, though—" Trevelyan saw that Ilaloa was sitting up. She trembled still, but the tears weren't running. He noticed that weeping didn't disfigure her as it does a human.

"Go easy on her," said Nicki quietly.

"I will." Trevelyan went over and sat on the desk, swinging his legs. The Lorinyan's violet eyes met his with a forlorn kind of steadiness. "Ilaloa," he asked, "do you want to talk about this?"

"No," she said. "But I will do so, since it is necessary."

"Good girl!" Trevelyan smiled. Looking on the warmth of his face, Nicki wondered how much of it was acting. "Just describe to me what the thought in Kaukasu was like. How did it feel? Did it say anything?"

"If you have never felt thought, I have no words."

"Oh, I have. It comes all at once, doesn't it? A main thread, but there are all sorts of little sidelines and overtones, hints, whispers, glimpses. And the whole thing is never the same; it's always changing. Is that right?"

She nodded. "As well as words can put it, that is right."

"Very well, then, Ilaloa. As nearly as you can, will you tell me what this thought you sensed was like?"

She stared before her, and the slim fingers gripped the chair arms until the knuckles stood white. "It was all at once," she whispered. "It came, pulsing, as if something lay under a pool and moved up, and then sank back into dark."

A shiver went across her. Sean started forward, but Joachim pushed him back. "It was of power, and scorn, and hugeness," she told them. "A hand gripping a universe, like iron. But slow, patient, watchful. And there was a shiningness against sky-black, a field of light, stars all around. They curved like a sickle to reap the field. And there was one star brighter than all, high and cold, and there was another shining coil which was so far away that the farness made me want to scream and—" She shook her head. "No," she breathed shakily. "No more."

"I see." Trevelyan clasped his hands and leaned forward, elbows on knees. "Do you think you could draw a picture of those stars?"

"A—picture? Why—"

"I'd like to put you under hypnosis, Ilaloa," he said. "That's just a sleep. I want total recall. You won't know it. And by that means I can take the fear from you."

She looked down, then up again, and her mouth quivered. "Yes," she said. "You may do that. I want to help you."

The hypnotism didn't take long. Ilaloa went under fast. Sean winced at the violence of her re-enactment, but the peace that followed was worth it. Trevelyan gave her a pencil and she sketched a star-field with swift assurance, adding the forms of nebulae and a section of Milky Way. The Coordinator took the paper and brought her out of the trance. She smiled sleepily, got up, and came into Sean's arms.

"It should be all right," said Trevelyan. "I think I removed the associated panic. It was due to sheer strangeness, not to personal menace." Then he turned away, and his features hardened with thought.

"What've we got?" asked Joachim.

"Well," said Trevelyan, "apparently these X beings think on a varying band and wave-form; Ilaloa caught only such fragments as were similar to her race's pattern. The fact may tell us something about the thinker—I'm not sure yet. What's more important is this star picture. It represents another region of space—presumably the home sky of "X.""

"Ummm, that's obvious." Joachim considered the drawing. "We've got a damn good clue, then. Let's see. The shiningness is a bright gaseous nebula, of course, and the remote spiral is probably the Andromeda galaxy. That very bright star could only be Canopus, if you're in the Cross region, and here's the same dent in the Milky Way you can see from here." He gestured to a view-screen overhead, blackness and the ghostly bridge of stars.

"In short," said Trevelyan with a note of triumph, "We've got a pretty good idea of where the enemy lives."

"Uh-huh. I think more can be done with this. Hey, Manuel!"

The young astrogator looked up. Joachim folded the drawing into a paper airplane and shot it over to him. "Find me this part of space as accurately as you can," directed the captain. "Use all our star tables and computers if you have to, but identify it within a centimeter of its life."

CHAPTER XII

TIME WAS LOST.

Within the ship, there was always light, cool glow in the halls and public rooms, someone walking by on an errand or sitting and waiting in patience. Darkness came only when switches were turned in the homes.

Outside, a night of stars, enormous and eternal.

There was no time. Clocks rounded a weary cycle, telling off the meaningless hours and days, but for man there was only waking and sleeping, eating, working, idling, waiting. The old dreamed of what had been and the young of what was to be, but the now was forever.

A few incidents were sharp in Trevelyan's memory. There were some of the talks he had with Nomads, Joachim before all, tales of faring in the cold Galactic splendor. There were his trips with Nicki, prowling the labyrinthine corridors of the ship.

There was the time a dark young man with unhappy eyes, Abbey Roberto, had searched out the

Coordinator and warned him that Ilaloa was a witch. Trevelyan remembered Sean's account of Roberto having overheard something about telepathy. There *had* been mutterings and sidelong glances when Ilaloa passed by. And the mounting tension aboard ship as they plunged into mystery could unsettle stabler minds than these.

At least the *Peregrine* had a fairly definite goal now. The point in space from which the sky should look as Ilaloa's vision said could be identified within a few tens of light-years. At full cruising speed, it lay about six weeks' journey from Erulan.

A month passed. It could have been a week or a century, but the clocks said it was a month.

They were in the park, four of them together talking and wanting companionship. Nicki sat crossed-legged beside Trevelyan, linking an arm with his. Opposite them was Sean, Ilaloa leaning against his side.

The park was the largest division of the ship from cargo space and, after the hyper-engines, the most impressive. It filled ninety degrees of hull curvature on the outermost deck, and its length reached a hundred and twenty meters from the bows. But that was necessary.

In the day of great cities, men had been caged in the stony, glassy mountains of their creation, and it was not strange that so many had retreated into madness. What then of humanity locked in a shell of metal and raw energy, between the stars? They could not have endured it without some relief, grass cool and damp underfoot, the rustle of leaves and ripple of flowing water.

This was the place of assembly, the captain speaking to men who stood on the wide green lawn in front of him. But just now there were only some children playing ball there. Otherwise the park was a place of trees, the trees of Earth, and of hedges, flower beds, fountains, winding paths and secret bowers.

Trevelyan and his party were in one of the bowers, leaning against the dwarf trees hemming it in. An oak spread above them, its branches dripping with heavy grapevines; and rosebushes and willows made a little grotto of the place.

A viewscreen opened on the outside. It sat vertically, like a window, and its metal outlines were drowned in ivy. Space loomed frightfully there, framed in a gentleness of leaves, ablaze with the diamond points of stars, falling outward to the uttermost ends of the universe. Ilaloa sat on the farther side of Sean, not looking at the screen.

They were talking of civilization. Always Nicki drew Trevelyan out, asking him about his home, and he was not loath to respond. He wanted the Nomads to understand what was going on.

"In some ways," he declared, "we're in a position like that of Earthbound man in, say, the sixteenth through early nineteenth centuries. That was a time when any part of the world was accessible, but the voyages were long and difficult and communications lagged. Transmission of information—the ideas, discoveries, developments of both home and colonies—was slow. Coordination was virtually impossible—oh, they did influence each other, but only in part. It wasn't even appreciated how foreign the colonies were becoming. North America was not England; the whole ethos became something else. If they had had radio then, even without better ships, Earth's history would have taken a fantastically different course.

"Well, what have we today? A dozen or more highly civilized races, scattering themselves over this part of the Galaxy, intercourse limited to spaceships that may need weeks to get from one sun to the next—and nothing else. Not even the strong economic ties which did, after all, bind Europe to its colonies. Cross-purposes are breeding which are someday going to clash—they've already done so in several cases, and it's meant annihilation."

"Hmm—yeah." Sean ran a hand through his unruly hair. The other arm was about Ilaloa, whose eyes were somber, and he saw that she was tensed as if waiting for something.

Nicki nodded toward the Lorinyan girl. " 'Lo is right," she said. "You do think too damn much, Micah, and you're too lonesome up there in your own head." She gestured at the view-screen.

"Look out there, Micah. That's *our* universe. We belong here. Forget your damned science for a while. Reach out and take the Galaxy in your hands!"

"A big Galaxy," he murmured.

"D'you think the Nomads don't know how big it is?" she cried. "You think we haven't spent our lives out here, seeing worlds beyond worlds and always new suns beyond those? The stars don't know we exist, and when we're dead they'll go on as they always did, as if we'd never been. But still we belong, Micah! We're one atom in the universe, but at least we're that much!''

She stopped, and a slow flush crept up her cheekbones. ''I'm really mouthy today,'' she said. ''Blame it on 'Lo. That way of talk she has is catching.''

He smiled, wordlessly.

''But I would not say such things,'' whispered Ilaloa. ''Your belongingness is not mine. Micah feels himself part of a pattern, a not-real, something like a thought in his head. And you of the ship think of fire and metal and that hollowness out there; to you life is just a stirring in dead matter. Oh, no!'' She buried her face against Sean's shoulder.

''And what do you think, then?'' asked Trevelyan. ''What is most real to you?''

She looked up again. ''Life,'' she said. ''Life that is in all space and time, the forces—no, the *is* and *becomes* that shapes itself. It—'' She stopped helplessly. ''You have not the words. You try to understand life, as if you could be outside it. But you cannot. It is not to be understood but to be known. Felt, and you not locked in a house of bone but part of it—like a river, and you are a wave which rises and will sink back again, but the river flows on.''

Sean stroked her hair. ''You say some funny things, sweetheart,'' he murmured. His lips brushed the smooth pale cheek.

''Bergson,'' said Trevelyan.

''Hm?'' Nicki raised her brows.

''A philosopher of Earth, 'way back when. He had ideas which sound much like Ilaloa's. But I doubt if he carried them out the way she could. Someday," he added thoughtfully, "I'd like to ask you about your people, Ilaloa. I've been so busy studying the ship that I've neglected you, but I think you could teach me something."

"I will try." Her voice was almost inaudible.

"Micah," began Nicki slowly, "are we Nomads so very different from your Union?"

He nodded. "More than you imagine."

"I mean—oh, we live differently, yes, but we're still human beings, from Sol to Galaxy's edge. And do we really think so otherwise?"

"Of course. We're all flesh and blood. What are you getting at?"

"The way you talked before, I thought you thought we'd become some kind of poison-breathing monsters. I was wondering, though, how you and I—our people, that is—could ever get along."

"Strife isn't necessary," he answered dully. "But as long as the two cultures exist, there can't be any real union. We live for things that are too different. Just remember what happened to some of those you adopted, or to Nomads who tried to settle down in a colony."

"I thought that was what you'd say." Slowly, Nicki withdrew her hand from his. He didn't move.

Sean stirred clumsily, "I think I'll stroll around the park," he said. "Come along with me, 'Lo, will you?"

They had risen, he and the Lorinyan girl, when they felt a tremor pulse briefly through them, a sudden nauseating twist.

"What the hell—!" Nicki sprang to her feet.

"The gravity-field generators—" began Sean.

Another surge came, shaking them. Their eyes blurred, and a huge windy sigh went through the leaves overhead. Voices lifted in shouts. Someone cursed.

"X!" gasped Sean. "They're attacking us!"

Trevelyan was erect now, standing behind Nicki and gripping her arms. "No," he answered. "A ship in hyperdrive *can't* be assaulted. It—"

Ilaloa screamed.

Looking in her direction, Trevelyan saw the stars waver in the view screen. There was a sheet of fire and the screen went dead. Smoke curled acridly from it.

Another wave and another, tossing them to the floor. Metal groaned. Trevelyan saw an oak branch snapped off and hurled across the shivering room. He scrambled back to a swaying stance. Nicki stumbled against him and his arms closed around her.

Lightning flared, a blue-white hell of electric discharge from wall to wall. After it came the thunder, booming and echoing within the hull like a great gong. The floor heaved underfoot. The light went out and there was lurid darkness torn by crackling arcs. The ship rang.

Through the tumult, Trevelyan heard the amplified voice as a distant cry: *"Micah! Trevelyan Micah, can you hear me? This is Joachim. Come up to the bridge and give me some help!"*

Lightning speared across the dark and the voice blanked out. A siren was hooting emergency stations, crazily, unnecessarily. A body crashed into Trevelyan and brought him again to the floor.

"Vortex!" he shouted. "We've hit a trepidation vortex!"

CHAPTER XIII

TREPIDATION VORTEX: *A large traveling force-field of uncertain origin and nature, manifested as a gravitational turbulence with gyromagnetic and electric side-effects. The name derives from the fact that the differential equations describing conditions on the fringes are similar to those for a vortex in hydrodynamics, as well as from the popular association with a maelstrom. These vortices are responsible for a number of phenomena, including trepidation of planets and other small bodies. The fluctuating forces they exert on spaceships, as well as the irregularities they introduce into hyperdrive fields, have violent consequences, the vessel often being destroyed or hurled far off course; doubtless the vortices are responsible for most otherwise inexplicable disappearances of ships. The best theory of the trepidation vortex is due to Ramachandra and proposes that local concentrations of nascent mass—*

Dictionary definitions! Was the lexicographer ever in such a storm?

Lightning sheeted through the room and thunder banged in its wake. By its glare Sean saw an uprooted tree falling, and rolled to escape it. The branches flayed off his shirt.

"Ilaloa!" he cried. "Ilaloa!"

He felt her in his arms and held her close, straining against the floor. It toned with a giant vibration through flesh and skull and brain. By another electric flash he saw Trevelyan grope across the park, Nicki clinging to his hand. A woman cried out. Then the reverberance of metal drowned human voices.

Induced currents— His body felt the heat under him, and he smelled the grass as it began to char. They couldn't stay here! The floor rocked, falling dizzily away and then rising to smash at his ribs. Shifting gravitation— "Come on, 'Lo, come on," he groaned.

They lurched up, clutching for each other. The darkness was a chaos of echoes, booming and banging, shriek, whistle, crack and crash. From some forgotten corner of his mind a memory was spewed up. You couldn't have an electric field inside a hollow charged conductor. The lightning discharges had been between non-conductors, trees, and these were down now. But there would be fire!

A heave and pitch sent him staggering. Broken twigs knifed his skin. He climbed erect again, leaning on Ilaloa—somehow she had kept her feet. They crawled over the tree.

Light was dimly reborn, blue fireballs created in

the air and drifting on its winds. He saw Ilaloa's face etched against the dark. She wasn't frightened now, but he couldn't read her expression.

A lightning ball swooped past, like a small sun. He felt a tingle in his nerves and every hair stood up by itself. Beyond the dull radiance was a howling night.

Someone blundered into him. He looked on a boy's distorted face. *"Have you seen my sister?"* The voice was dim under the endless metallic roar. Hands clutched at his shoulders. *"Where's Janie?"*

"Come with us—" Ilaloa reached for the boy. He was suddenly gone, whirled away. Sean saw pain in her face, then the murk closed in again.

Gravitation tilted horribly. He went to his knees, sliding down a curve of hot steel. He fetched up brutally against a wall. Ilaloa was still with him, arm locked in arm.

Another globe of ball lightning hovered by. He saw a man gasping toward them. His face was hollow with terror and he drooled from an open mouth.

"Abbey! Abbey Roberto!" Sean shouted through the sundering roar of metal, hardly knowing he did.

The man stumbled closer. There was a knife in his hand, and Ilaloa gasped. Abbey snarled, swinging the blade at her.

"Witch! Damned murdering witch, you did this!"

Ilaloa grabbed for his knife wrist. He struck at

her with the free hand, a buffet that sent her to her knees.

Sean's world reddened. He stepped above Ilaloa's crouching form, driving a knee into Abbey's stomach. The other man choked and thrust at him. Sean caught the descending arm in his hands, and twisted the knife loose. Abbey clawed for his eyes. Sean stabbed him.

The lightning ball exploded, thunder and fury and a rain of fire. Its glare was livid over the trembling, staggering walls. Sean crouched with Ilaloa, holding her close and waiting.

The restless forces had thrown Trevelyan across the room, to skid along toning metal and strike a fallen tree. He came out of it in a minute, focusing blurred vision on the riven ship. Nicki was holding his head, frantically. Gathering himself, he willed the pain out of his consciousness.

"Come on," he said. The iron roar trampled his words underfoot. "Come on, let's go."

She helped him up and they made a slow way through skirling, ringing murk. By the brief glare of spinning fireballs they saw a wreck of tangled branches, splintered trunks, and tumbled bodies. Now and again they passed an injured human, but there weren't many in sight. The Nomads were meeting this well, thought Trevelyan; they were going to emergency posts without stopping for panic.

The end of the park was ahead now. Nicki lurched, and he caught her, pulling her to him. For a moment they stood face to face in raving gloom. Then a fireball blew up, flaring the incandescence of hell across the ruins, and he saw her limned against night, eyes on his and lips parted, hair tossing in the wind.

Thunder followed, a doomsday bank and roar. He kissed her.

It lasted for a long while. Then they drew apart, staring at each other without real understanding, and ran on toward the bridge.

There was a flash suspended over the astrogation desk, a well of radiance and all the rest an enormous moving dark. Joachim's battered face was sliding shadow and dim highlights. His roar lifted above the sundering echoes: "There you are! What in Cosmos' name can we do?"

For just an instant, Trevelyan recalled that something of the processes in a vortex had been known to Sol for almost a hundred years. But the frontier wanderers, to whom that knowledge could be life, had never heard of it. "Let me see your instruments," he shouted.

Outside was utter black, the viewscreens dead, but the ship's meters still registered. Needles flickered insanely across dial faces. Gravitational and electric potentials, gradients, magnetism, gyration, frequencies and amplitudes—he took it in at a single hurling glance, and his trained subconscious computed.

"We're still on the fringes," he cried. "But we've got to get clear. Components of the vibration have the ship's resonant frequencies. They'll shake us apart, atom by atom!"

Steel groaned under his voice.

"If we get the ship as a whole in phase with the

major space-pulsations— Can you signal the engine room yet?''

Joachim nodded.

"All right. Pulse the hyperdrive, sinusoid—here, I'll give you the figures." He scribbled on a page of the log. Joachim tore it out and punched the keys of the emergency telewriter.

The ship howled! The floor fell away beneath Trevelyan; he was floating free, falling and falling endlessly through darkness. Then a titan's hand grabbed him and threw him at the wall. He twisted in mid-air, drilled reasonless reflex, and landed on his feet. Wave after wave beat through the ship. The floor buckled. He heard the snapping of girders.

He shouted for Nicki, stumbling up and reaching into a night that shuddered. Metal belled and gonged around him. "Nick! Nick!"

Thunder bawled through the ship. He heard the hoof-beats of ruin galloping across the desk. The clangorous war cry filled his universe.

And died!

Slowly, slowly, the vibrant metal shrilled into silence. He stood listening to that waning voice and wondered if this were death. He seemed to be afloat in endless space and time. He groped into thick night, not sure whether he was blind or not, and heard the cries of men about him.

"Nicki!" he sobbed.

"We're free." Joachim's voice came quiet, resonant, from far away. "We're free of the storm."

The hyperdrive went off. Joachim must have signaled for that. They hung in normal state, open space. The burned-out viewscreens functioned as ordinary ports, and Trevelyan saw the stars.

By the hazy sheen of the Milky Way, river of suns spilling across infinity, he saw Nicki. Remembered words came to him, as if someone else were speaking into that great silence. *"Hast thou commanded the morning since thy days; and caused the dayspring to know his place? . . ."*

Joachim stared out at heaven. "Where are we?" he asked.

"The constellations don't look any different! No, wait, they do a little." Ferenczi was at another port, his body black against the Milky Way. "That ridge shape wasn't there before."

Joachim pointed to the lurid brillance of Canopus. "We're still in the general region," he said. "But vortices have been known to throw ships—any distance."

"There's a sun pretty close to us. Look over here."

Joachim went to where young Petroff Manuel stood, legs spread wide as he stared down into the port under him. Yes, a nearby star, a reddish one maybe only light-hours off. Its luster hurt his eyes.

He blinked, looking away from it to the soothing gloom of the bridge. Gravitationally overhead, a port glittered with stars. He glanced at it and grew stiff.

"Thunder and fury!" he breathed. "Lads, come over here. We've arrived!"

They followed him with their eyes and saw the configuration in the sky. A filamented web of light sprawled in the sickle-shaped curve of a dozen bright stars. "The nebula!" shouted Joachim.

"The storm threw us to where we were going!"

Ferenczi's teeth gleamed in his shadowy face. Joachim turned from the frosty nimbus and his voice snapped. "Work to do, lads."

He saw Trevelyan and Nicki by one of the ports. They were looking at each other, eyes into eyes, hands clasped. Briefly, Joachim smiled. Life went on. Whatever happened, life went on.

"All right, break it up over there," he called. "Save it for later."

"We will!" There was a sob of laughter in Nicki's voice.

Slowly, Trevelyan turned and walked over to the captain. Nicki followed, brushing back her tangled hair with hands that trembled a little. Joachim was already on the intercom. Some parts of the ship's communications system were out, but he was able to call most stations. The answers came shakily, not fully believing in salvation.

"All right," Joachim faced back to his officers. "We're banged up, but we seem to be in running order. Karl, take charge up here, and if anyone calls asking for orders, you give 'em. Meanwhile, straighten up this mess a bit. Find out where we are, as nearly as you can, and study that red sun. I'm going on a little tour of inspection. Want to come, Micah?"

"Yes, of course. Not much I can do here."

"You did enough, lad. If it hadn't been for you, this boat'd be split right down the middle."

"Well—" Trevelyan's bruised lips managed a smile. "Coordinators do come in handy."

Joachim looked archly at Nicki. "Make nice pets too, huh?"

She didn't answer. She was wiping the blood from a cut in Trevelyan's face.

They went down the companionway. It had been twisted into an S, and its lower end had torn loose from the deck plates. Beyond the hall, their wide-angled flashlights touched on havoc. The park was a heap of windowed trees, shattered fountains, and blackened grass. A thin haze of smoke hung in the unmoving air.

"Ventilators dead hereabouts," noted Joachim. "That'll rate high on the fix-it list."

They walked the length of the park. A man lay sprawled against a dwarf oak, eyes bulging sightlessly and neck awry. Beyond, there was a woman with a broken leg, but already someone was tending her. It was quiet here, little sound or motion.

"Your people rally well," said Joachim, shrugging. Then: "Hullo, somebody seems unhappy."

He led the way, pushing through a torn hedge into what had been an arbor. Ilaloa was crouched there, shuddering with sorrow. Sean sat by. Near them, was a dead man with a knife in him.

Joachim bent to look at the corpse. "Abbey Roberto," he murmured.

"He tried to kill Ilaloa," said Sean, tonelessly.

"Hmm, yeah, I reckon he had some funny ideas. But so do ship courts. However"—Joachim pulled out the knife—"Roberto must have got his when he stumbled onto a jagged edge of something." He wiped the knife clean and returned it to Abbey's sheath.

"Thanks," said Sean.

"Forget it, lad. We've got troubles enough as is."

They rounded the ship, looking in everywhere and gathering a picture of the damage. Casualties were fairly light—a few dead, a score or so seriously injured, the rest only superficially hurt. There was a tremendous wreckage of the more fragile equipment, but nothing irreparable; and the essential structure of the ship was intact. Joachim left a trail of organized working parties.

"We should be able to get under way again in a few hours," he summed up, "but it'll take longer to get us back in fighting shape. We'll have to find a place where we can hide out for a while to complete repairs."

"It doesn't have to be a planet, does it?" asked Trevelyan.

"Well, just about. If nothing else, I'd like to get some excess mass for the converter—we're low on it, and you know how hungry a ship in hyperdrive is. And there might be demands from our weapons, too. Pick up a few tons of something, maybe a couple of meteors. Then our food plant is banged up, too. We can live off preserved stuff if we must, but green vegetables from an E-planet would help morale until we get our own tanks producing again. And we need to recalibrate our instruments, too. I'll bet the storm raised merry hell with 'em. That calls for observations taken inside a planetary system. And—"

"Never mind, I see your point. Go to it. Nicki and I'll lend a hand here."

"Sure, lad. See you." Joachim stumped off toward the bridge. The lighting had been restored by now, and his stocky shape looked oddly alone as it dwindled down the metal length of hall.

Nicki turned back to Trevelyan. "It's not possible," she said softly.

"What isn't?"

"That I could be so happy."

He smiled and kissed her, taking his time about it. He thought briefly of Diane, back on Earth, and hoped she wouldn't be lonely long.

The ship had run into a vortex—why? Such things did happen, of course, but . . . Did X have his home behind a screen of storm? No, that couldn't be. A vortex traveled at high speed; it was completely improbable that X's sun should have precisely the velocity of this turbulence.

Could the thinker in Kaukasu have deliberately given Ilaloa a pattern? Following the most direct route to the sector revealed would indeed have led the *Peregrine* into the storm.

He turned the data over to his subconscious for whatever it could do with them, and gave himself to the manual labor of repair. The Nomads were shaken by their experience, but were recovering.

There were several hours' rest yet, though. Trevelyan saw Nicki to her door but didn't enter; then he returned to his own room and threw himself into bed.

He awoke when the siren wailed its signal and men grew rigid at their posts.

"Hoo-oo-oo . . . hoo-hoo . . . hoo-oo-oo . . . hoo-oo-oo . . . hoo-hoo-hoo– Stand by! All hands stand by battle stations! Strange spaceship detected where no spaceship has any business being!"

CHAPTER XIV

STANDING ON THE bridge, where Joachim had hastily summoned him, Trevelyan looked out to a great sweep of stars and a single planet. The sun was a ruddy disc; with the glare filtered out by restored viewscreens, he could see the dark whirlpools of spots across its photosphere. Like most giant stars, it had a big family of planets.

It was a J-planet, though, a colossus more massive even than Jupiter; its atmosphere a hell's broth of hydrogen, methane, ammonia, and less well-known compounds. It was a beautiful sight, hanging there in space, a flattened globe of soft amber radiance, belted with greens and blues and dusky browns, one red spot like a pool of blood. The man discerned three moons close enough to show perceptible crescents.

"It doesn't make sense!" Joachim stared at the flickering meters which told of a spaceship nearby. At this range, the neutrinos given off by its engines were detectable, and there was the "wake" of gravity fluctuations by the drive, and even the faint pull of its own mass. The *Peregrine's* maltreated instruments might be somewhat inaccurate, but there could be no mistaking their message.

"It doesn't make sense!" Joachim repeated. "We know there's nobody here with atomic power."

"X," said Trevelyan. "Suppose they have a patrol vessel in each system of their empire—or at least in many systems within the volume they regard as their own. By mounting detectors in suitable orbits around this star, they would automatically know of our arrival. So their ship could run at high acceleration to intercept us."

"Yeah, yeah, I suppose." Joachim lit a clay pipe and drew heavily on it. "And we're in no condition to fight. Should we clear out as of now?"

"Well, we came here to study the Great Cross beings."

"Uh-huh. We can always go into hyperspace. All right, let's wait."

The *Peregrine* went into free fall, curving slowly down toward the J-planet. The bridge was still. Only the muted purr of engines had voice—warmed up, waiting. Down the length of the ship, men stood by guns and missile racks. Armed boats hovered in space a few meters from the vessel. Sean would be piloting one of them, Trevelyan thought.

The communications man looked up from his set. "I've tried the whole band," he said. "Not a whisper of a signal. Shall I call them?"

"No," said Joachim. "They know we're here."

He took a restless turn about the bridge and came back to give Trevelyan a defiant glance. "Your Union exists for peace," he said. "What if we have to fight these otherlings?"

The Coordinator's green eyes were steady and

flat. "If we are attacked without provocation, we can fight as much as necessary to save our lives. But we have to find out *why* we are assaulted. Their reasons may be completely valid in terms of their own thinking."

"And my epitaph will be: *'Here lies a law-abiding citizen!'*"

Petroff Manual's shout ripped the quiet. "I can see 'em now!"

They hurried to his screen and peered out at darkness. There was a tiny point of reflected red light moving swiftly across the stars. It grew even as they watched. Joachim turned the screen to full magnification, and the image of a spaceship was before them.

It had the elongated shape necessary to any hyperdrive ship, where field generators must be mounted fore and aft. But it was no vessel of man's building. The cylinder was beveled into flat planes; the stern bulged, and the nose held a spear-shaped mast of some kind. Its metal was a coppery alloy, flaming ruddy in the harsh sunlight, and they could see that the hull was patched and pitted—*old*.

Trevelyan sucked a hissing breath through his teeth. Joachim gave him a long stare. "You know that design?"

"*Tiunra.*"

"Huh?"

"I've seen pictures of their ships."

"The same otherlings who lost boats out here in the Cross, four hundred years ago—"

"X is Tiunran?" murmured Ferenczi.

"It isn't logical," replied Trevelyan shakily. "The Tiunrans were explorers and scientists. They were neither physically nor culturally fitted for conquest. And when a technology has advanced to the point of interstellar drive, it doesn't *need* an empire.''

''X,'' said Joachim, ''has one.'' The ship was drawing closer, matching velocities as it approached. He stepped down the magnification.

''Maybe!'' snapped the Coordinator. ''We don't know yet.''

The stranger was only a hundred kilometers or so from the *Peregrine* by now, visible to the naked eye as a blink of light. In the magnifying screens it was a grotesque spindle in the sky. Joachim's stubby fingers punched signals to his crew on the communications board.

A meter jumped and an alarm buzzed. Electronic computers flashed orders to the robot pilots. Joachim read the signals. ''That's a self-guiding missile on its way,'' he said. ''No parley, no warning, no nothing—just a fission warhead tossed at us. You still want to play peacemaker with 'em, Cordy?''

Trevelyan didn't reply. He was staring out at the ship, wondering what crew it had. They could be anything; there was no telling. And there were so few who could see past ugliness, strangeness, hostility, to the ultimate kinship of life. *Stranger, enemy, kill it!*

Light glared soundlessly in space. The *Peregrine's* computers had intercepted the missile with one of their own. Another followed it, to be snatched up by a gravity beam and hurled back at the sender. And now the *Peregrine* threw her own barrage, swift gleams and hellish fury exploding short of the target.

Constellations swung insanely across the viewscreens as the *Peregrine* dodged a patterned flight of shells. The crew didn't feel it; the internal gravity generators automatically compensated for acceleration. But the crew only watched dials, fed the guns and missile racks, tending a robot's brain as it fought for them. Flesh and blood and the human mind were too slow and weak for this battle.

Strange combat, thought Trevelyan. It was a flickering shadow play of stars and bursting light, a chess game played by machines while men stood watching. The only sound was the irregular hum of the gravity-drive engines and the faint *whoosh-whoosh-whoosh* of ventilators.

No—wait. He heard another noise, a creak and groan in the girders of the hull. Overtaxed by the storm, not yet inspected and repaired, the structure was giving before the stress of swinging that huge mass through the maze of thrust, feint, parry, and dodge.

And Ferenczi's bearded hatchet face was grim as he looked up from the computer indicators. "We're lagging," he said. "Our detectors and calculators aren't fast and accurate enough. Before long, one of those shells or missiles is going to hit us."

"I thought so." Joachim sprang to the communications board and grabbed the radio mike. "All boats return! All boats back to the ship!"

This was the danger point. The little spacecraft

had to come back, enter the boathouses to be under the drive field's action. And as they dropped in, the *Peregrine* had to ease the violence of her maneuvers lest she hurl them through her own outer shell. At those instants, the enemy might—

Joachim studied the detector dials. "They're easing up. Not throwing as much at us. *Why?*"

Trevelyan looked out to the stranger. "Maybe," he said softly, "they don't want to annihilate us."

"Huh?" Joachim's expression was almost comical. "But what—"

"They didn't assail us with more than we could handle. They're going slow now, just when any determined commander would be tossing all he had at us. Are we simply being warned off?"

A buzz cut across his voice. "Everybody in," said Joachim. He threw over the engine-room signal switch. "So long, friend."

This close to star and planet, the hyperdrive built up with distressing irregularity. Trevelyan hung onto a table top, fighting his stomach. It was over in minutes and the red sun was dwindling astern. Space glittered chill around them.

Joachim wiped his face. It was wet. "I wouldn't want to go through that again?"

Ferenczi's tones fell dry. "We've taken astronomical data on this whole region. There's a Sol-type star about ten light-years from here."

"If the others are there, too—" began Petroff.

Joachim shrugged. "We have to go somewhere. All right, Karl, give me a course for that sun."

"The aliens, if they are the same as X, know we favor GO dwarf stars," said Trevelyan. "Has it occurred to you, Hal, that we're being herded?"

Joachim regarded him strangely. "It's a thought," he said slowly. "But we haven't much choice in the matter, have we?"

Trevelyan left the bridge and returned to his room. Bathed and freshly clothed, he went in search of Nicki. He found her waiting at the door to her apartment. For a moment he stood looking at her; then she came to him and he drew her close.

After a long time she sighed and opened her eyes. "Let's go to one of the boathouses," she said. "Only place we can have some privacy. The park's full of working parties. But I'm off duty just now."

He glanced toward the apartment, but she gestured him away. "Sean and 'Lo are in there," she told him. "He was out in his boat, you know, gunning missiles, and it doesn't have the computers or the power to escape one. I thought 'Lo would go to pieces."

They went down the corridor. Her fingers tightened convulsively about his. "I thought we were all done for," she said with sudden harshness. "I knew we were all done for," she said with sudden harshness. "I knew we couldn't stand off a real attack, and you were on the bridge and I couldn't be there—"

"It's all over. Nobody was hurt."

"If you were killed," she said, "I'd steal a ship and go hunting for the killer till I found him."

"You'd do better to help correct the conditions that led to my being killed"

"You're too civilized," she said bitterly.

The ancient war, he thought, the immemorial struggle of intelligence to master itself. Nicki could never stay on Earth. As if reading his mind, she said slowly, "If we ever get clear of this, we're going to have to make some decisions."

"Yes."

"There isn't a chance you would stay with the ship?" she asked wistfully. "Be adopted?"

"I don't know. I wasn't brought up for that. To me, life is more than starjumping and trading. I can't escape myself."

"But you wander a lot on your jobs," she said. "I could go along. Don't you ever need an— assistant?"

"When I do, I get one, another Coordinator, most likely an otherling. But—we'll see, Nicki."

They went down a companionway, through the lower level and into one of the boathouses. There wasn't much room between the boat and the sur- rounding fliers, but they were alone, standing in metal and looking out a viewscreen at the stars.

She turned on him fiercely. "You're wiser than I am. You know better what will come of this. Only I'm not going to set you free. Not ever."

"If you went from the ship with me," he asked, "wouldn't you ever miss it?"

She paused. "Yes. They're stupid and narrow and mean here, sometimes, but they're my people. I'd do it, though, and never be sorry."

"No," he agreed, "You're not one to back down on a decision."

He looked out at the steely light of stars. "We'll wait and see."

The *Peregrine* went on across space. Her crew worked hard, repairing, restoring—preparing for whatever might lie at journey's end. Joachim drove them ruthlessly, less to get the job done than to take their minds off danger.

Near the end of the third day, they went out of hyperdrive and accelerated inward. The instruments peered and murmured, and clicked forth a picture of the system. Eight worlds were detected. One of them circled its primary at a distance of slightly over one astronomical unit, and the ship moved toward it, matching velocities as she neared. Telescopes, spectroscopes, and gravitometers strained ahead during the hours of flight.

There was no sign of atomic energy; and as the *Peregrine* took up an orbit around her destination, there was no other ship. The crew gathered at the viewers for a look at the planet.

It was Earthlike to many points of classification. It was a serene and lovely sight as they approached; against the naked blaze of the stars, it was a sign for peace.

Joachim directed an orbit some thousand kilometers up, using gravity drive to remain above a chosen spot. "It looks pretty," he said. "We'll send down a boatful of scouts. I think Ilaloa should go with them. That telepathy or whatever-it-is of hers may pick up something. Then Sean will have to go, too. And you, Micah; you're trained to spot aliens."

"I'm quite willing," said the Coordinator, "but if I go, you'll have to tie up Nicki to keep her aboard."

"That wouldn't do any good unless we could gag her, too. All right, take her along."

CHAPTER XV

LANDING ON A planet of this sort was a stylized procedure which Trevelyan watched with interest. Nomad doctrine closely paralleled that for a Survey vessel; but the equipment used was not so elaborate and some items of sheer ritual had crept in.

Two fliers went ahead, each bearing two men, plunging down from the sky at reckless velocity. The region chosen was an island about a thousand kilometers long and three hundred wide, a place of hills and forests and broad river valleys. The fliers cruised just above the treetops for a good half hour, men peering with eyes and instruments. There was no sign of habitation, no metal, no building, no agriculture. Geosonic probes revealed that the ground was firm thick soil over normal bedrock and water tables. No outsize animals, or even large herds, were spotted. It was safe to land.

The boat followed more slowly, settling to the ground with a crew of twenty, and the fliers dropped to rest on either side of her. Men stood by the guns, but that seemed a meaningless gesture. The landscape beyond the ports was utterly peaceful.

"In the name of Cosmos, sanctuary," said the boat's captain, Kogama Iwao, formally. "All right, boys, hop to it."

Ten spacesuited men clashed down their helmets and moved to the airlock. The inner door shut on them and a high whine signaled the sterilizing radiations and supersonics which filled the chamber while the outer door was open.

A sunbeam touched Ilaloa's hair with molten silver. "It is free and light out there," she said. "Why do you hide from it in dead steel?"

"It looks nice," agreed Nicki, "but you can't tell. There might be germs, molds—a hundred kinds of death. Those leaves might be poisonous even to touch. We're not afraid of hungry monsters, 'Lo. It's easy enough to handle them. But sickness that gets inside you—"

"But there is no danger," said the Lorinyan. Bewilderment still overrode her voice. "This is the home of peace."

"We'll find that out," said Kogama brusquely. "What's the word on the atmosphere, Phil?"

Levy glanced at the dials of his molecular analyzer, which had sucked in an air sample. "No poison gases in any quantity, except of course the usual tinge of ozone," he replied. "A few bacteria and spores, naturally. I'll tell you about them in a minute."

The analyzer buzzed to itself, scanning the organic structure of the microscopic life it had trapped. A cell of such-and-such nature must feed on a fairly definite range of tissues in a certain manner, and give off predictable by-products. One by one, the specimens were tabulated until the verdict stood: nothing airborne that was harmful to man.

By that time, the armored gang was back, carrying samples of soil, plants, water, and even a couple of insects. They were made aseptic in the airlock before entering. The prophylaxis was too brief to affect anything below the surface of their specimens, and Levy's crew got to work with practiced skill.

Analyses disclosed Earth-type life, similar down to most of the enzymes, hormones, and vitamins; nothing to cause disease in man. Marooned humans could live here indefinitely.

Kogama chuckled at the final word and rubbed his hands. "All's well," he said. "We can go out and relax, I suppose."

"You're aware, of course, that you haven't taken a fair sample of this planet's life forms?" asked Trevelyan.

"Oh, no doubt there are things which can hurt us—venomous plants, for instance. But nothing we can't handle, I'm sure."

Trevelyan nodded. "What's your next line of study?"

"Sending parties out to hike around. Let's see—" Kogama looked out the western port. "Say five hours to sunset. That's time enough to get a pretty good notion of the layout here. Want to go, Micah?"

"Of course."

"A few'll have to stay by the boats, just in case. Might as well be me in that group. I'm lazy." Kogama belied his yawn by snapping a string of orders. Sixteen people were organized into four parties, each assigned to walk in a definite direction and come back before sunset by another route. Sketch maps made from the air were provided, to be filled in by the hikers as well as possible, and samples of anything unusual were to be brought back for study.

Trevelyan leagued himself with Sean, Nicki, and Ilaloa to make one group. The three humans wore coveralls, boots, skin-tight gloves, wrist radios, guns and canteens and medic kits at waist. Ilaloa had flatly refused to wear extra clothing.

"Let her have her way," said Kogama. "If something poisons her, it'll be a handy way for us to learn what's dangerous."

"There is no danger," insisted Ilaloa. She sprang from the airlock to the grass and stood almost shuddering with ecstasy. Slowly, she lifted her hands and closed eyes to the sun.

Nicki regarded the slim white form with a touch of envy. "Wish I had her nerve—or foolishness," she said. Then, looking about her and drawing a deep slow breath: "It's beautiful. It's as beautiful as Rendezvous, and I never thought there could be two such planets."

Trevelyan had to agree with her; a man could make his home here.

As he went toward the forest, Trevelyan became aware of its noises. They were like Earth's in their myriad small whispers, but he missed the songs of grasshopper and meadowlark. Even the wind in the leaves had a different sound.

Ilaloa danced before her companions, laughing aloud, wild with the sudden joy of release. Like a wood nymph, thought Trevelyan—and any moment Pan might come piping from the brush.

The four went up the hill slope, guiding them-selves by a gyrocompass powered from the boat.

"It could be a park," said Nicki, after a long silence.

Trevelyan blinked in surprise. Something about the landscape had been haunting him; now some-thing chilled in him. "Who," he asked slowly, "is the caretaker?"

"Why"—Nicki's eyes regarded him with puzzlement—"nobody. It was just something I said."

"It *could* happen this way," he answered flatly, "but life is usually a struggle for place. This looks—landscaped!"

"But that's silly, Micah. Nobody lives here. Not even X would make a park of a whole world which he didn't inhabit."

Trevelyan looked ahead of him. Ilaloa was standing by a tree whose branches were heavy with dusk-colored fruit. Sean tried to stop her as she plucked one, but she laughed and bit into it.

"That's pretty careless," said Trevelyan. Nicki, arm in arm with him, felt his muscles grow rigid.

Sean was still protesting as the two approached. Ilaloa held the fruit to him. "It is good," she said. "There is sunlight in it."

"But—"

"Try it, my dearest." Her voice softened. "Would I give you that in which there was harm?"

"No. No, you wouldn't. All right, then." Sean accepted the gift and tasted. A slow expression of delight crossed his thin features.

"It's delicious!" he called to his companions. "Try some."

"No thanks," said Trevelyan. "Leave un-analyzed stuff alone. Even if it doesn't hit you right away, it might have slow-working effects."

They came out in an open meadow. Trevelyan shot an animal, a small quadruped. Its green color proved to be due to algae living in its fur.

"Hey!" yelled Sean. "Hey, look over here!"

Trevelyan followed him to the tree on the pasture's edge. It was a graceful thing, not unlike a poplar, swaying and whispering in the wind. But the leaves had prominent veins and—

And they would glow in the dark, Trevelyan knew. This was one of the species reported by Survey, the same life-forms impossibly scattered over half a dozen worlds. And the pieces of the puzzle fell together.

"It's a torch tree!" exclaimed Sean. "A torch tree just like on Rendezvous—"

"X," whispered Nicki. "X has been on our planet, too." Her hand stole to her gun.

Their wrist radios shattered stillness with a jagged urgency: "Attention, all parties! Attention! This is Kogama at the boat. Natives approaching!"

Trevelyan lifted his eyes to Ilaloa. He did not see victory on her face. It was more like a sudden grief. "Yes," she said.

"They're humanoid all the way down the line." Kogama's voice rattled above the talking forest. "White skins, bluish-white hair, males, beardless—all naked and weaponless, coming slowly out of the woods— *No!*" It was almost a scream. "They can't be! Attention, all parties, attention! These are—"

Kogama's voice faded in a gasp, and then there was silence.

Trevelyan's hand rested on the butt of his gun, but he didn't draw. "What was done, Ilaloa?" he asked, very quietly.

"A sleep gas blown down the wind." Her voice was small and toneless. "They are not hurt, only sleeping."

"*Ilaloa—*" Sean started forward, his gun half out. "*Ilaloa—*"

The natives stood before them, a few meters away on the edge of the meadow. *They must have trailed us without our knowing,* thought Trevelyan. He looked them up and down, the superb naked forms of half a dozen men, white as marble statues come to life. Their silver hair streamed in the wind, past the cleanly chiseled faced of Hellenic gods, tossing over broad shoulders. One of them carried a thing like a big gray egg, a few metallic insect forms hovering about it.

"Stand back!" Sean had his gun free now, pointed shakingly at the strangers. His cry was animal. "Back or I'll shoot!"

A slow smile curved the lips of the men. The one with the egg spoke in human Basic, accented but fluent, like music from his throat: "If I tell the dwellers in this nest to sting you to death, they will do so. Or if I drop the nest, they will. Put down your weapon and listen."

Nicki raised an arrogant head. "We'll fill you with holes first."

"You do not understand." Ilaloa stepped in front of the humans. "Your kind is sundered from life, and bears within it the fear of death and the longing for death. We have neither. Throw down your guns."

Trevelyan sighed. At this moment, he felt only a colossal weariness. "Go ahead, do it," he ordered. "Our getting killed wouldn't help matters any, nor do we know how many more of— these—there are watching us. Put down your weapons, Sean, Nicki." He dropped his own into the grass.

The stranger who bore the egg of death nodded. "That is well."

CHAPTER XVI

ODDLY, IT WAS on Ilaloa that Trevelyan's gaze rested. The pride had fallen from her like a dropped cloak, and she took a step toward Sean with her hands held out to him.

The Nomad turned, making a sound like a strangled sob. He went to Nicki as if she were his mother, and she held him close. Ilaloa stood for a small moment watching them. Then she slipped into the forest and was lost.

She still has that intuition of the right thing to do, thought Trevelyan. *Now isn't the time for her.*

Slowly, he faced around to the tall being who had spoken. That one was carefully setting the gray nest into a tree crotch. His hands free, the captor smiled again. It made his face a warm dazzle. "Welcome."

Trevelyan folded his arms and stood regarding the other from expressionless eyes. "That's a curious thing to say to us."

"But it is true," insisted the allien gently. "You are guests here. It is not a euphemism. We are genuinely glad to see you."

"Would you be glad to see us go?" asked Trevelyan wryly.

"Not immediately, no. We should like to give you some understanding of us first." The handsome head lowered. "May I perform the introductions? This planet we call Loaluani, and we are the Alori. That word is not quite equivalent to your 'human,' but you can assume for the present that it is. I am designated—named Esperero."

Trevelyan gave the names of his party, adding, "We are from the Nomad ship *Peregrine*—"

"Yes. That much we know already."

"But Ilaloa didn't say— Are you telepaths?"

"Not in the sense you mean. But we were expecting the *Peregrine*."

"What are your intentions toward us?"

"Peaceful. We—a few of us who know the art—will take your boat back to the ship. The crew will not suspect anything, having received no radio alarm, and being too high for telescopic observation of what has happened. Once in the boathouse, we shall release the sleep gas, which will be quickly borne through the ventilators. All the Nomads will be taken down here in the boats. But no one will be harmed.

"Do you wish to come with us? Our party is going toward that section of the island where we feel you will be most comfortable. Your fellows will be landed there."

"Yes—yes, of course."

Nicki flashed Trevelyan a crooked grin. She walked a little behind him, one hand on Sean's shoulder. The Nomad moved like a blind man. Trevelyan stayed beside Esperero, and the other

Alori flowed on either side. *Flowed*—there was no word for the rippling grace of their movements, soundless under sun-dappled shadows. The forest closed in around them.

"Ask whatever you like," said Esperero. "You are here to learn."

"How did you arrange for us to come? How did you know?"

"As regards Lorinya, or Rendezvous as you call it," said Esperero, "we had colonized it for about fifty years when the Nomads came, and we watched and studied them for a long while. Their language was already known to some us, and we had means of spying on them even when none of the Alori were present." As Trevelyan lifted his brows, the alien said only, "The forest told our people."

After a moment, he went on: "Four years ago, Captain Joachim was heard to mention his suspicions of this part of space to others. It was logical that he would sooner or later investigate it, and we determined to get an agent aboard his ship. Ilaloa was chosen and trained. When the *Peregrine* came back this year, it was not hard for her, using the empathic faculties of our people, to find someone who would take her along. I do not know yet just what she did to influence your journey—"

"I can tell you that." Trevelyan related what had happened in Kaukasu. "Obviously there was no thinker behind the walls. She's a superb actress."

"Yes. Ilaloa gave you a star-configuration such that your most direct route from the planet to here would run you into the storm."

"M-hm. And I suppose she'd been given post-hypnotic blocks so that she responded as desired even under hypnotism?"

"Did you try that? Yes, of course, they would have guarded her in any way possible."

"Except against the storm itself," said Trevelyan grimly. "That nearly annihilated us."

"If so," said Esperero, "we would at least have removed one potential enemy."

There was an unhumanness in his tone. It was not cynical indifference, it was something else—a sense of destiny? An acceptance?

"However, you did survive," continued the Alorian. "Our idea was to drive you to a colony so that we might capture you, as we have done. There were half a dozen equally probable colonies, and each of them has been ready for your arrival. I happen to have been the one whom you—picked, shall we say?" His smile was impish, and Trevelyan couldn't help a one-sided grin.

"I should have known," he said ruefully. "If I'd thought to investigate Ilaloa at all, I would have seen the truth."

"You are not a Nomad, are you?"

"No. The Nomads didn't stop to check the facts or reason the thing through, and I had too much else on my mind. But if I'd known that the Lorinyans were supposed to be mere savages . . . !

"Ilaloa spoke nearly perfect. Basic, with an unusual vocabulary even for a human. She knew obsolete words like 'sickle,' which she could only have found in literary references—and she didn't read much, if at all, on the trip. And when we tried to argue each other's philosophies out, she often had very sophisticated remarks. I assumed that she came from a rather high culture which had had a good deal to do with the Nomads.''

"That was true enough," said Esperero.

"Yes, but to the Nomads the Lorinyans were primitives. They— Never mind.'' Trevelyan sighed. Every time you thought you had reality expressed in a system you stumbled against a new facet. The sane man must be always distrustful of his own beliefs.

"You will not be harmed," said Esperero.

The hills rolled away under their striding feet, woods and shadows and the slowly declining sun. Trevelyan saw animal life everywhere, climbing up the trees, crawling over the ground, rising heavenward on glorious wings. He heard a song which was all whistles and trills, happy lilt in a bower of blossoms. The Alori bent their heads to listen, and one of them whistled back, up and down the same scale. The bird replied differently. It was almost as if they spoke together.

They passed a large mammal, like a graceful blue-furred antelope, one horn spiraling from the poised head. It watched them out of calm eyes. Didn't the Alori hunt at all?

Nicki spoke behind Trevelyan. "Micah, we Nomads should have realized that the Lorinyans weren't native to Rendezvous. Every other back-boned animal there has six limbs."

Trevelyan turned back to Esperero. "Where did you come from originally?"

"Alori. It is a planet not far from here, as astronomical distances go. But it is very unlike your Earth. That is why our civilization has developed such a different basis from yours that—'' Esperero paused.

''That one must destroy the other?'' finished Trevelyan softly.

''Yes, I believe so. But that need not mean physical destruction of the beings who have the culture.''

''You're not going to meddle with *my* mind!'' Nicki snapped.

Esperero smiled. ''No one will try to force you to anything. We ask only that you see for yourselves.''

''In what ways are you so different?'' asked Trevelyan.

''That will take a long time to explain,'' said Esperero. ''Let us say that your civilization has a mechanical basis and ours a biological. Or that you seek to master things, where we wish only to live as part of them.''

''Let the differences go for now,'' Trevelyan said. ''If you don't go in for inventiveness—the mechanical kind, anyway—how did you get off your home planet?''

''There was a ship that landed, long ago, an exploring vessel from Tiunra, with strange, furry little beings in it—''

''Yes, I know.''

''The Alori are a unified culture. They evolved as one, whereas your kind did not. That is again a reflection of the gulf between us. Our people had already climbed the mountain peaks that reached above Alori's shielding clouds. They had seen the stars and, by methods different from yours, had learned something about them. They made the

Tiunrans prisoner and decided that they must defend themselves.''

"The Tiunrans hadn't hurt you, had they?" asked Sean.

"No. But—you must wait, must see more of our life before you can understand. . . . The Alori took the ship and went out among the stars. Many of them lost their minds to that strangeness and had to be taken back for healing. But the rest went on. They encountered other Tiunran ships—they captured three.

"No more Tiunran ships came here, but it was realized that many races would be starfaring and some inevitably come to us. And the very fact of their building spacecraft meant they would be of the same alien stamp. We began colonizing habitable planets throughout this region. There were not many like Alori, which is an unusual type, but we found beauty in worlds like this, too. We spread the life we knew between the stars, so that the universe was no longer quite so cold."

Esperero paused. The sun was getting low; this planet had about a twenty-hour day. "I think," he said, "that we will camp soon. We could easily go on through the night, but you will wish to rest."

"Go on with your history," urged Trevelyan.

"Oh, yes." A shadow crossed the graven face. "As you like. We found, in our explorations, that we were almost unique. You can understand that that increased our uneasiness for the future. We colonized all untenanted worlds habitable to us, bringing Alorian life-forms and modifying the native ecology as much as necessary. A few other planets—" He hesitated.

"Yes?" Trevelyan's voice held ruthlessness.

"We exterminated the natives. It was gently done. They hardly knew it was happening, but it was carried through. We needed the worlds and the natives could not be made to co-operate."

"And you say man is dangerous!"

"I never accused you of being unmerciful." Esperero shook his head. "Perhaps later you will understand how it is."

Trevelyan's will surged out to clamp on his feelings. Man's history had been violent. If he respected intelligent life today, it was because he had learned by fire and sword and tyrant's gibbet that he must.

"All right," said the Solarian. "Continue."

"At present, we have colonized about fifty planets," went on Esperero. "It is not a large domain, though it covers a considerable volume of space by virtue of our planets being widely scattered. And we cannot build machines ourselves. That would destroy the very thing we seek to preserve.

"We watched the Union grow. I need not tell you in detail how we studied it. Among so many races, it was easy to pose as members of yet another. I myself have spent years wandering about your territories, investigating them in every aspect. We have seen your gradual expansion toward us and known that sooner or later you would discover our existence. Against that day we have prepared. We have seized spaceships which took orbits unawares about our planets, thus adding to our fleet. In Erulan, we buy ships outright."

"The man there," said Trevelyan slowly, "told

us that humans bought the ships for gold. He was sure they were humans."

"Yes. Other races have joined with us and taken on our life. Among them have been crews, and descendants of crews, from those spaceships we took."

"And you expect *us* to—" Nicki's whisper held a note of terror.

"You will not be forced," said Esperero.

They came out on the brow of a hill and looked across deep dales to the horizon. The sun was setting in a rush of color.

"Let us rest," said Esperero.

His followers moved quietly to their few tasks. Some of them disappeared into the woods, to return presently bearing fruits and nuts and berries and less identifiable plants. Others broke off gourds, which proved to be hollow, and large soft leaves.

Trevelyan fingered one of the gourds curiously. It was perfect for its use—a line of cleavage made it easy to open; a spike on the bottom could be driven into the ground. There was even a handle. "Do these grow naturally?"

Esperero chuckled. "Yes, but we first taught them to do so."

"How about shelter?"

"We will not need it. We do have tree dwellings, but we can sleep outside. Would you really rather lock yourself in with your own sweat and breathing?"

"N-no, I suppose not. If it isn't raining."

"Rain is clean. But you will understand later."

Twilight deepened to a silky blue. The Alori sat

in a grave circle. One of them said a few words, and the others responded. There was ritual in it, as in everything they did—even the handing out of the food was somehow ceremony.

Trevelyan sat by Nicki, smiling. A milk-filled nut which was its own goblet was given him, and he touched it to hers. "Your health, darling."

"You may eat and drink without fear," Esperero told him. "There is no fear on this planet—no poison, no hungry beasts, no hidden death of germs. Here is the end of all strife."

Trevelyan tasted of what was offered him. It was delicious, a dozen new and subtle flavors, textures that his teeth liked, nourishment coursing along his veins. Nicki joined him with equal fervor.

Sean stood leaning against a tree, looking over the moon-flooded valley. He felt hollow inside, as if nothing were altogether real.

Ilaloa came to him. He saw her white in the moonlight, and she slipped up till he could have touched her. He didn't look at her, but kept his eyes on the valley. Here and there in its darkness the torch trees were like spears of radiance.

"Sean," she said.

"Go away," he replied.

"Sean, may I talk to you?"

"No," he said. "Begone, I tell you."

"I did what I had to, Sean. These are my people. But I wanted to say that I love you."

"I'd like to break your back," he said.

"If you wish that, Sean, then do it."

"No. You're not worth the trouble."

She shook her head. "I cannot quite understand

it. I do not think any other of the Alori has ever felt the way I do. But we love each other, you and I.''

He wanted to deny it, but words seemed futile mouthings.

''I will wait, Sean,'' she said. ''I will always be waiting.''

CHAPTER XVII

THE NOMADS had been taken to a valley on the island's northwestern coast, surrounded by hills and opening on the sea. When Trevelyan's band got there, the initial confusion was over. Fifteen hundred people had settled down to a dazed waiting for whatever came next.

Joachim met the new arrivals on the valley's edge. "Been waiting for you. One of the natives told me you'd be coming down this trail."

"How did they know that?" asked Nicki. Esperero's men had left them a few kilometers back, pointing out the route for them to follow.

"I don't know," shrugged Joachim. "Telepathy?"

"No," answered Trevelyan. "Incredible as it seems, I'm beginning to think that the forest here forms a communications network."

"The original grapevine telegraph, huh? Well, let it go. We had a little trouble to start with, but those boys can handle themselves." Joachim clicked his tongue admiringly. "Their judo starts where ours leaves off. No harm done, though, and the crew's pretty well quieted down now."

"You've been given living quarters?"

"Yeah. Such of the natives as know Basic told us

they'd evacuated this bunch of tree houses for our benefit. They said they wanted to be friends, even if they couldn't let us go back to bring down the human race on 'em. Since then, nobody's been around. Tactful.'' Joachim looked keenly at Sean. ''If I was you, lad, I wouldn't show myself either for a few days.''

''I understand,'' said Sean.

''They'll realize it wasn't your fault, and cool off, after a while, but I came to warn you. I know of a couple of trees away from the main village where you can stay.'' The captain turned to the Coordinator. ''You got any ideas as to just what we're supposed to do?''

''Settle down. Learn more about the setup before attempting anything.''

''Uh-huh. Snatched my ship right out from under me! Transplanted me like a vegetable! It's enough to drive a man from drink.''

Trevelyan studied the Alori houses with more than casual interest. They were reminiscent of the naturally hollow trees in which the Nerthusian aborigines dwelt, but incomparably farther advanced. Each bole contained a smoothly cylindrical room that was a good seven meters across, light and airy; the wood hard and beautifully grained. There were windows which could be closed by transparent flaps of tissue that were part of the tree; a similar, heavier curtain served for a door. The floor was carpeted with a mosslike growth whose springiness held a living warmth.

A couple of extruded shelves formed table space; there was no other furniture, but the floor made a restful bed. Vines tendriled about the trunk looped inside with a riot of flowers, among which hung bladders that glowed after dark with cool yellow light. These could be "turned off" by drawing their own loose husks about them. From one wall a hollow, inward-growing branch yielded clear water when squeezed, a natural drain below taking the run-off. Next to the tree grew a bush whose waxy fruits were an excellent soap surrogate; the other needs of the body could be taken care of in the boundless forest.

Trevelyan moved into an isolated tree, Sean and Nicki taking its neighbors. His own tastes not being elaborate, he didn't miss the ordinary appurtenances of human life.

The village, he found, was actually an extensive settlement, comprising some five hundred units—more than enough for the Peregrines, especially when one could live just as well outdoors. The dew took a little habituation; thereafter, even the trees seemed cramped and stuffy.

Pets had also been taken from the ship. It was strange to see a terrier barking at a rainbow-winged insect, or sleeping in the shade of a half-meter broad flower. Soon after the humans' arrival, some of the Alori returned with a courteous offer to bring whatever else was desired from the *Peregrine*—now in free orbit just above the atmosphere. Joachim got a list of wants from his people, mostly tools. It seemed to amuse the Alori, but they brought the things. Joachim listed his own whiskey, tobacco, and a few pipes at the top.

The Nomads began to relax. It was evident by now that no harm was intended by their captors, who were apparently content to leave them to their own devices.

Trevelyan met several of the Alori often. He used to walk into the forest, alone or with Nicki. When he felt like talking to one of the——natives—— it wasn't usually long before somebody showed up. Esperero seemed to be his special mentor.

"What plans do you have for us?" asked the Coordinator.

Esperero smiled. "I have said we will not coerce you—directly. But you are a restless folk. Most of you will soon begin longing for open space again."

"So——?"

"So I anticipate spasmodic activity among you. Handicrafts will resume, for one thing. The forest offers many possibilities to the creative mind, and our people will give advice when needed. That will help break down the unfriendliness toward us."

"Some of those projects you may not like," said Nicki.

"I know. For example, men will begin to think of hunting. They will make bows and other weapons. But they will find that the animal life has disappeared. In like manner, their other unsuitable ambitions will be frustrated."

"And if they turn against you?" asked Trevelyan.

"They will know better than to try organizing a war party against a whole planet. But Nomad culture, like any other, is the product of an environment and its necessities. Here the physical environment, open space, is gone. The planet will absorb them.

"They won't become Alori. This generation,

whirling out of shadow into the unreal moonlight, soaring as if they had wings. In and out, back and forth, and the glowing fireballs were with them, birds with luminous feathers darted between their flying white forms, and the music sang of springtime.

Now it became summer, growth and strength, a giant rush of rain; clouds burst apart, sunlight speared through, it blazed across an endlessness of ocean. Land raised green from the sea, surf white against its cliffs, trees lifting heavenward and striving their roots into the planet. An animal roared, shaking his horns in might and splendor. The dance leaped into fury.

It became slower, stately, the passion of laden boughs and the land turning gold for harvest. The death of summer lay in hazy distances and cool high nights. Far overhead, a wedge of birds flew southward, and their cry was a lonely song for wanderers.

Trevelyan wondered what the music was to the Alori. To him it was Earth, the sweeping years and the final sinking back against the strong bones of the world. But he was human; he held Nicki close.

Winter. The dancers scattered like blowing leaves; moonlight fell chill on emptiness, and the music keener with hungry winds. Cold gripped the planet, daylight like steel, night of bitter stars, hissing snow and the southward-grinding glaciers. Aurora shimmered weirdly over the face of heaven. One dancer came forth and stood for an instant as if in despair. Then she stamped her foot, once, twice, and began to dance the end of all things. Trevelyan saw that it was Ilaloa.

She danced slowly at first, groping as if through mists and flying snow. The music lifted again, sharp and savage; she danced faster, fleeing, cowering, the flutter of broken wings, hunger and ruin, cold and death and oblivion. She danced with a wildness and a hopelessness that numbed him to watch. The music was like the crash of glaciers trampling mountains underfoot, spilling across broad plains and proud forests. It was like winter gone mad, wind and snow, night and storm, calving icebergs in the north and whelping hurricanes in the south. The world groaned under its weight.

The storm died. Slowly, the dancer moved away, slow as life fading from creation. When she was gone, there was only the heavy dead thunder of the ice and sea, mourning wind and the sun smoldering to ash. It was over.

And yet there was fulfillment in it. Life had been, had struggled, and died. Reality *was*—no man needed more.

When silence and moonlight came back, the Alori did not stir. They sat for a long while without moving or speaking. Then, one by one, they rose and disappeared into the shadows. The festival was over.

Nicki's face was white under the moons. They were sinking. Trevelyan saw with dim surprise. Had it only been one night?

When they got back to the Nomad camp, Joachim said the marriage service over them. Afterward there was a feast and merrymaking, but Trevelyan and Nicki didn't stay long.

CHAPTER XVIII

THEY WANDERED from the settlement, two of them alone, and ranged about the island. There was no hurry. When they found a place they liked especially well—a sandy cove, a hidden glen, the lonely heights of a mountain—they stayed until a vague restlessness blew them on.

Trevelyan wanted to learn more about the Alori civilization. But to know it, he had to contemplate it.

Often they encountered Alori in the woods, or stumbled onto one of their villages. They were always made welcome and their questions were freely answered. As he became more adept in the language, he took to thinking in it, for no speech in his civilization could fully handle the new concepts.

In so far as Alori culture could be compared to any human society at all, it was Apollonian—restrained, moderate, everything balance and order and adjustment. It had little use for the aggressive individual; nevertheless, each individual was fully developed, very much himself, free to choose his own endeavor within the pattern.

It was not a perfect society, even by its own standards. Utopia is a self-contradictory dream. There was sorrow here, as elsewhere in the universe; but grief was a part of living.

Nor was the Great Cross domain a place of mindless contentment. In its own way, it was as scientific a culture as Sol's. But the underlying theoretical foundation was altogether alien. The Alorian mind did not analyze into factors; it saw the entire problem as one unified whole. When the question itself was incomplete, a man would say he had not taken all the relevant data into consideration; an Alorian would say the organization did not feel (look? seem? There is no equivalent word in Basic) right.

On the other hand, the Alori were fumble-fingered when it came to the simplest compound machines. The most intelligent of them could not understand an ordinary radio transceiver, and they were astronauts entirely by rule of thumb. They had only the vaguest notion of the atom, none at all of the nucleus. General field theory was so alien to them as to be repellent.

More and more Trevelyan realized what an implacable hostility this people had—not to being within his civilization, but to the civilization itself.

"If they don't think they can stand competition," he said once, "their own philosophy ought to tell them that their way of life is unfit and should go under. But they *can* take it if they have to. They have knowledge we would pay anything for. And there wouldn't even be competition in the normal sense, not when every planetary system is or can easily be made completely self-sufficient."

"I don't know," answered Nicki. "Does it matter very much?"

He looked sharply down at her. "Yes," he said at last. "It does."

They were standing on the southern coast, atop a rocky headland. Before them lay the sea; a fresh damp wind blew in under the high sky, tossing Nicki's dark yellow hair.

"It's almost as if they were fanatics, like the militant religions of the statist tyrannies of old days on Earth," he said.

"So one way of life gives place to another," said Nicki. "Is that worth killing about?"

"It's more than that. War corrupts as much as power. When I told you once there was no reason for interstellar empire, I ignored one possibility because I didn't think it existed any more. Empires are a defense. If someone attacked for ideological reasons, the planets assaulted would need a tight organization to fight back."

"But would they—the Union—have to fight? Wouldn't it be easier to give in?"

"It's not a question of whether they would *have* to fight or not. The fact is that they would. A society tends to be self-maintaining, especially against outside pressure." Trevelyan laid a hand on his wife's shoulder. "This doesn't sound like you, darling. You used to be a regular firebreathing dragon."

"I wasn't happy then," she said. "But this—it's so quiet and beautiful, Micah. It—" Her voice trailed off.

"Don't you want to go starjumping again?"

"Oh, yes. Someday. But why not for the Alori?"

"Because when the last comes to the last, Nicki, we're humans. Man has always been a fighter. We can take what is good for us, but it must be on our own terms."

"You've got an answer for everything, haven't you?"

He grinned. Nicki was still a spirited wench.

Later he made open inquiries of the Alori, and fitted their polite but unyielding answers into the pattern he was assembling in his own mind. They saw the universe as an organic whole in which everything *must* belong. Division was madness.

The mechanical civilization of the Union was abhorrent to them.

In spite of that, they could have left the Union alone; but its drive was outward, and they lay in its path. Their knowledge was beyond price to Man; he would want to *know*.

And contact would be deadly for them. Intercourse would modify both cultures, but the Alori could not stand change.

"I can understand it," said Nicki softly. "Suppose somebody caught me, Micah, and used one of those personality machines on me so I wouldn't love you any more. I'd know that when they were finished, it would be all right. You wouldn't mean anything to me then. But I'd fight it every step of the way. I'd be gouging eyes and kicking low and screaming my throat out."

He kissed her, there in the rustling darkness of the forest.

The suggestion that the Union would be sympathetic and willing to isolate the Great Cross met only a courteous skepticism. And Trevelyan had to admit that was justified. Such an isolation would only be a temporary expedient. Sooner or later, on one pretext or another, there would be contact. By that time, the Union would be too strong to cope with. The Alori meant to act now; they had already been acting for some time.

If they won an absolute victory, the prospect was bearable. The dreadful thing was the chance of their trying and losing. Then there would be two civilizations plunged down toward night.

And Trevelyan admitted to a prejudice in favor of his own society. His race had created something unique, and he didn't want it to go for naught.

He didn't hate the Alori; more and more he came to love them. If their achievement died, a light would go out in the universe. There wholeness-principle was something which had never been properly formulated in Union logic. It should be possible to make integrators which would not fit isolated data together but consider a local complex—society and its needs, physical environment, known scientific laws—in its entirety. Alori science, with the knowledge it had of the nervous system, would indicate ways to build such computers.

He sat with Nicki on a small skerry to which they had swum. You could never be sure how much the forest heard.

"We have to escape," he said. "We must warn the Union of what's brewing here, and tell it that the answer to its biggest question is waiting.''

''What will happen then?'' Her words were low, hardly audible in the ripping wind.

''The Alori will accept a *fait accompli*,'' he answered. ''They'll give in and make the best of it. It's not as if we came to enslave them.''

''We haven't the right,'' she whispered.

''What are they planning for us?''

''Oh, I know—but do two wrongs make a right?''

''No,'' he said. ''But this isn't a matter of ethics. We're going to stay free—and that's that.'' His gaze was challenging. ''Don't you ever want to go out to the stars again? Not on a mission, not with a purpose, but because it's your own life and you do as you choose with it?''

She lowered her eyes. A bird winged overhead. It was native to the planet, not yet brought into the symbiosis; it was hunting for something to kill.

''The world is as it is,'' he said. ''We've got to live with that—not with the world as we think it should be.''

She nodded, very slowly.

CHAPTER XIX

WHERE THE valley opened on the sea, there was a wide beach sloping from high grass-grown dunes to the steady wash of the tides. Joachim's party found themselves a place to sit and made a crescent, facing inward toward the captain. He stood up, a burly, hairy man darkened by the sun, and fumbled a cold pipe in his hands. Slowly, he scanned the ring of faces and bronzed bodies.

There were some twenty-five Nomads present, besides himself and Trevelyan. The Coordinator sat next to the skipper, one arm about Nicki's waist. She leaned close to him and her look was unhappy. The rest were strained with expectation. Sean was here, plunged into the gloom that had been his since he arrived on Loaluani.

Joachim cleared his throat. "All right," he said. "I think we can talk freely. No big fat trees to crawl up on us and eavesdrop. This one has been sort of sounding people out, and got the impression that all of you here are pretty much of a mind. Then Micah came back and built a fire under me, so I called this picnic. I think all of you got the idea." He paused, meeting their eyes. "I want to get out of here," he said then. "Anybody want to come along?"

They stirred, and words muttered between them, an oath snapped out, fists clenched. "It's not too bad a life," went on Joachim, "but it's got its drawbacks. I reckon they're different for each of you."

"It's plain enough," said Petroff Dushan. "I want to go starjumping. This planet is—dull!"

"Yeh," growled Ortega. "Just a park. Every morning I check my skin to see if moss ain't started growing."

"Remember Hralfar?" asked Petroff Manuel wistfully. "There was snow. You could feel the cold, like the air was liquid. You wanted to run and shout, and you could hear sounds for kilometers around, it was that quiet."

"Give me a city," said Levy. "Bars and bright lights, noise, a wench and maybe a good fight. If I could sit in the Half Moon on Thunderhouse again, by the Grand Canal—!"

"A place with some spice to it," said Mac-Teague. "The flying city on Aesgil IV, and the war between the birds and the centauroids. Some place *new!*"

"Once we're converted to this Alori life," said Joachim, "they'll let us spacefare—for them."

"Yeah. But we never will be, and you know it," said Kogama. "And who ever heard of a Nomad traveling for somebody else? We go where we please."

"All right, all right," said Joachim. "I know how you all feel."

Thorkild Elof compressed his mouth bleakly. "We'll end up marrying within our own ship," he said. "I've already noticed boys and girls going together, because there's no one else: It's obscene.''

"Are they going to make Alori of us?" cried Ferenczi. "It's been done to the others. The old *Roamer, Tramp, Tzigani, Soldier of Fortune*—they aren't any more! Their crews aren't Nomads"

"Yeah," Joachim nodded. His face tightened. "They took *my* ship and *my* crew. They've got to be paid back for that."

"Just a minute," interposed Trevelyan. "I've explained—"

"Oh, sure, sure. Let the Cordys handle the Alori. I only want to get loose again." Joachim turned his pipe over and over in stubby fingers. "I've burned up all my tobacco and killed all my bottles. The Alori don't drink or smoke."

"It's all very well to talk," said Elof impatiently. "But we're down here and the *Peregrine* is up there. "What can we do about it?"

"Things." Joachim sat down, crossing his legs. "I've gotten you people together so I could be sure you were all with me." He sucked hard on the empty pipe. "Look, this one's been asking around among the Alori. They're very frank and polite, you've got to admit that. They know I don't like being here, but they also know I can't jump into space by my own legs—so they answer my questions.

"Well, the *Peregrine* is the only star ship around, for parsecs. Her boats were flown to a small island about twenty kilometers northwest of here. The Alori don't need 'em, so they're just sitting there. Some kind of guard is mounted—

plants or animals or something that won't let a human land without an Alorian's say-so."

"Wait a minute!" exclaimed Petroff Dushan. "You don't mean we should snatch us an Alorian and make him—"

"Wouldn't work," said Ferenczi. "These natives just aren't afraid to die. Anyway, I don't think we could capture one without all the damned woods knowing it and bringing the whole island down on our necks."

"Please," said Joachim. "My idea isn't that crude." His gaze turned on Sean, and he went on quietly: "Ilaloa's been around a little."

The young man's face flushed. He spat.

"Now don't be so hard on the poor lass," said Joachim. "She only did her duty. This one saw her a couple of times flitting around, and has never seen anybody so woebegone. We got to talking and she kind of poured out her troubles. She loves you, Sean."

"Huh!" It was a savage grunt.

"No, no, it's a fact. She belongs with Alori, but she loves you, and knows you're about as unhappy as you can get. And I think she's been a bit— corrupted by us, too. A few drops of Nomad have gotten into her blood. Poor kid."

"Well, what am I expected to do?" snapped Sean.

"Go to her. Take her to a place where you can't be overheard and ask her to arrange our escape."

Sean shook his head unbelievingly. "She wouldn't."

"Well, there's no harm in trying, is there? Her only alternative is to take some kind of psychological treatment to get you out of her mind, and she doesn't want to do that.''

''I understand,'' murmured Nicki.

''B-but she'll know I'm lying!'' protested Sean.

''*Will* you be lying? You'll say you still care for her and want to take her away if she'll help. I think that'll be the truth.''

Sean sat still for a long while. ''Do you think so?''

Joachim nodded. After a moment he added slowly, ''You might bear this in mind, too. If we do get away, this whole business will have worked out very well. A menace will be converted to a profitable enterprise. I think people will feel pretty kindly toward 'Lo.''

''Well—I—''

''On your way, lad.''

Sean stood up. He was shaking, ever so faintly. He turned and walked stiff-legged from the gathering. Nobody looked after him.

There was silence, wind and surf and the high crying of the birds.

Ferenczi said, ''It'll only be us here who make the break, eh?''

''Yeah. A bigger bunch would be risky. We can take the ship back to Nerthus. Hard work and short rations, but we can do it.''

''I was thinking about the others. They'll be hostages here.''

''I asked 'Lo about that, and what she said bore out my own hunch. The Alori don't do things without a purpose. They won't mistreat our people when they've already lost the game.'' Joachim got to his feet, stretching. ''Any more questions? If not, the meeting's adjourned until we know better where we stand. Avoid the natives, all of you. They'll sense your excitement. Let's get up a snappy game of volleyball to calm us down.''

Trevelyan stood with his arm about Nicki, looking over the beach. A few hundred meters off, Joachim's ball game got under way.

''What are you thinking of, Micah?''

He smiled, ''You,'' he said. ''And your people.''

''What of us?''

''You know the Service doesn't like the Nomads. They're a disrupting influence on an already unstable civilization. But I'm beginning to think that a healthy culture needs such a devil.''

''Are we so bad, we starjumpers?''

''No, you aren't that either. You aren't necessarily cruel to anyone. You have brought as much good as evil to the planets you visited, I think.''

His lips brushed her hair, and he caught the faint wild fragrance of it. ''I'll have to report back home,'' he said, ''and you'd like to visit Sol anyway. But after that—Nicki, I'm not sure yet, but I think I'll turn Nomad myself.''

''Micah!—Oh, my dearest!'' She held him desperately close.

''Peregrine Trevelyan,'' he murmured, as his mind raced on. This was his answer. The integrators would have to give a final verdict, but he believed he had found the way. Pure Nomad? No—but with his abilities, he would eventually become a power among the ships and influence what they did. And other Coordinators would be adopted, too.

They would give Nomad life a direction and a

restraint it lacked and needed, quietly, without disrupting its spirit.

Sean walked down the beach until he was alone between the forest and the sea. He climbed a dune, and stood looking out over the huge sweep of loneliness. Grass grew thin and harsh here, cutting at his bare legs. He shaded his eyes with one hand, looking at the shoreward march of grass where it blended into meadow and woods.

She came to him, walking timidly out of the forest. A few hundred meters away she paused, tensed for flight as if he had a gun. He stood watching her, his hands hanging empty. She ran.

He held her close to him, murmuring wordlessly, stroking the wind-whipped hair and the fine blue-veined skin, and let her weep herself out. Only then did he kiss her with an overwhelming gentleness. "Ilaloa," he whispered. "I love you, Ilaloa."

Her eyes were blind and wild, staring up at him. "You cannot remain here? You must go?"

"We must go," he said.

She looked away. "These are my people."

"It's not as if they would be harmed," he told her. "I have my people too. And they're yours as well."

"I could be treated. I could be healed of you."

He let her go. "Then do it," he said bitterly.

"No." Her lips were parted wide, as if she couldn't breathe. "No, that would be against life, too. I cannot."

"Is your life so much better than ours that it has to destroy us?" he asked.

"No." She laced her fingers together, twisting them around each other. "I think you are right, Sean. This is a dark and empty world—universe—we have to find what warmth we can."

She straightened and faced him. Suddenly her tones were clear. "I will help you if I am able."

CHAPTER XX

TWO NIGHTS later a gale blew from the southeast, out of the sea and over the island and out to the water again. Trevelyan heard it whistle as if it were calling him. He looked at Nicki, and she was very close and dear in the warm yellow light of his home.

She smiled, and it struck him with a hideous chill that she might be killed in the escape. But she would not hear other than that she should be with him.

The tree was snug, a hearthfire in an endless hooting dark. Seated on the mossy floor, he felt the slight tremble of it under the thrust of wind. Nicki started as the door curtain was pulled aside and flapped thunderously in the blast. Joachim stood there, fully clothed, his mantle drawn hard about his bearlike form. There was a recklessness in his eyes which they had never seen before.

"All set, folks," he said. "Come on to the beach. I'm passing the word." He nodded and was gone again; the darkness gulped him down.

Slowly, Nicki stood up. A tremble ran over her, and the blue eyes were haunted. She smiled, stroking one hand along the smooth wall of their home. Then, shaking her head so the tawny locks flew: "All right, Micah, let's go."

Rising with her, he stepped over to the shelf on which their belongings lay dustily forgotten.

"Before we go," he said, turning to Nicki, and kissing her.

When he stepped out, holding Nicki's hand, the blackness was like a rush of great waters. He heard the trees shouting; the wind snarled in their branches and they answered with a gallows groan.

They stumbled to the beach. When they came out on the shore, the wind was a blow in the face. Briefly, the ragged clouds tore open to show a half-moon flying between far pale stars.

Most of Joachim's party was already assembled, standing there waiting. The moonlight glistened frostily on the blades of knives and the heads of hunting spears, forged during the long days here.

They were standing in a damp gully where the river crossed the strand. A boat lay there, brought down from the woods by Ilaloa. Trevelyan reached out and touched the hull with a feeling of awe.

The boat was long and narrow, with a single mast—fore-and-aft sail and a jib, dark green—and a rudder and a small cabin. But she was a living tree, fed by sea minerals and earth laid in the bottom.

He saw Ilaloa, seated near the tiller. She was holding Sean close to her, as if she were already drowning. "Everybody's here, I reckon."

Joachim's voice was almost lost in the wind. "We'd better get going. I'm not so sure the Alori haven't some notion of this caper."

The boat had to be taken past the surf. Trevelyan splashed in the shallow river between grunting, cursing Nomads he could barely see. The hull was cold and slippery under his hands.

He felt the keel grate on a sandbar at the river mouth. Now—heave! Over the bar and into the surf! It rose swiftly as he waded out. The offshore wind flattened it, but he felt a vicious undertow yank at his legs.

"Cram 'er through!" roared Joachim. "Cram 'er through!"

Trevelyan hurled his muscles against the solidity of hull. His feet groped for a hold, lost it; he clung to the gunwale and then a giant's hand scooped him up. Water exploded over his head. A million thunders banged in his skill. They were in the real surf now!

The boat staggered. Trevelyan held on with fingers that seemed ready to rip from their sockets. A buffet sent him choking away, lungs aflame. He gasped, kicking with his feet, driving the boat outward.

She lay in pitching sea. A hand caught Trevelyan's hair, and the swift bright pain of it stabbed his mind back into him. He splashed against the heaving gunwale, grapped the rail, and pulled himself over. Turning, he stooped to help the next one.

The moon broke out again and he looked on an immensity of tumbled waters. To windward the land was a bulking shadow, black against moon-limned clouds. Inboard was a jammed mass of faces. He could barely hear the voices over the screeching wind and thunderous waves. Joachim stood upright, legs planted far apart, stooped over as he counted.

"One missing." He rose, peering into the dark swirl over the side. "MacTeague Alan gone. He was a good lad."

Slowly, he turned to face Ilaloa at the tiller. His hand lifted and swung down again. She nodded, a fey figure under the moon, and spoke to Sean. He and a couple of others fought the sails up.

The boat leaped! Her mast, which had been swinging crazily against the sky, heeled over so that Trevelyan thought she must capsize. The boom reached far out, almost at right angles to the lean hull, and the living ropes hummed. Water slanted icy-white from the bows, the wake coiled in shattered flame behind her, and she ran!

Trevelyan gasped, shaking his drenched head with wonder. "We made it," he breathed. He didn't quite dare believe it yet. "We made it."

Nicki hugged him, wordlessly. They crawled over their fellows, into the bows where they could see ahead. Spindrift stung their faces, but they looked over the sea and were glad.

The clouds were breaking up and the halfmoon, as big as Luna at the full, was dazzlingly brilliant. But it was straight ahead, to the northwest, that Trevelyan and Nicki stared. There lay the boats and the way home.

Joachim crept up to the bows, saw the two sitting there, and smiled. Turning, he made his way back sternward, checking on his people. No casualties so far, except poor Alan. Joachim wondered how he was going to tell it to the boy's father.

When he came to the stern, he saw Sean and Ilaloa helping each other steer. It was hard to figure how the girl kept her bearings without a compass, but she was doing it. The shore was already lost to sight; they were walled in ringing, sundering darkness. The tiller threshed, fighting like a live animal. Sean and Ilaloa were on either side of it, shoulder against shoulder, hands interlocked on the rod. The man had a strained look, but the captain had seldom seen such inward happiness.

He approached closer, hanging onto the rail with one hand and bending near so they could hear him call. "How's it going?" The wind yelled around his words.

"Pretty good," answered Sean. "We should raise the island soon. We could see it now if this were daylight."

Joachim leaned on the pitching bulwark, and looked down the length of the vessel. Strange that she wasn't shipping water—no, the water came inboard and was soaked up, blotted away; a fine rain sprang from the boat's sides, back down into the sea. She did her own bailing, too.

He looked over the sea as if he stood on a mountain. Overhead was a sky of flickering candle-stars and cloud streamers; under and around him the swooping, trampling, shouting sea, everywhere the wind. It might have been across light-years that he saw the hazy form of the other boat.

He gripped Ilaloa's shoulder so that she cried out. Slowly, he pointed, and she and Sean followed the line of his arm.

She stood for a bare second, not moving. He had seen a man once with a bullet in his heart, not yet aware that he was dead, standing just that way.

Joachim leaned over to shout in Ilaloa's ear: "Would anyone else be sailing on a night like this?"

She shook her head.

"Well," he said between his teeth, "hang on to your heads, lads, we're going to make a run for it."

As they mounted another crest, he saw the island. It was hard to gauge distances, but that sheer loom of rock couldn't be far now. Peering into the blast, he made out the other vessel. It closed the gap rapidly, quartering in from portside stern. No windjammer, this; the Alori had sent a real longboat after them. It was big and high-stemmed, no mast, and it was drawn by something that swam. He could only see the great white curve of a back rising from the waves, the thresh of its tail and now and again a monster fluke.

Canst thou draw out Leviathan with a hook? . . . Will he make a covenant with thee?

Ilaloa said something to Sean, who nodded and gestured to Joachim. A few rags of words came to the captain's ears: "—take rudder—reef—" He came around and closed hands on the kicking bar. Sean groped to the boom lines. The island was very close now, standing in a white flame of surf. They had to go around it, no doubt, tack—in this weather?

The sail slatted and banged, and the boat yawed, coming around on another tack. It was clumsy handling—Ilaloa could have done better, but she had inexperienced help. They lost most of their forward speed. The Alori vessel drew closer; it might only be a few hundred meters away now. Joachim saw the tall forms of her crew standing in the bows. He had a notion one of them was Esperero, but he couldn't be sure.

The island was a mountain before them. Joachim saw the surf that geysered under its cliffs and felt his heart stumble. The Alori boat pulled in, almost even with them now, though a good fifty meters lay between. Joachim looked at the seabeast's back and the tail that ripped the water.

No—not yet, by heaven! The sailboat sprang forward. Surf was just ahead of her now; he felt her lurch with its shock. A wave rushed in over the bow, thundering along the length of the hull, and then the keel slammed against a reef.

Ilaloa pointed wildly over the side. *Jump! Jump!* He stared for a dumb instant. The living sail tore across, and rigging snapped like rotten twine. He eased himself overboard.

There was bottom a meter down. This must be the shallows. And, he thought with sudden glee, the sea monster couldn't swim in here!

Trevelyan and Nicki joined him, standing in water that clawed at them and broke over their heads. A woman fell, going under. Trevelyan grapped her arms, helping her. Nicki took her by the dress, and they splashed slowly to shore.

Ilaloa stood there, Sean beside her, at the head of a trail winding up the cliff face. She gestured back those who would have climbed it. The crew stood waiting, jammed together.

Trevelyan looked past the smoking surf, out to sea. The Alorian boat was drawing up alongside the reef, where it shelved abruptly off. They were here and the spacecraft were only meters away . . .

He caught his emotions. Ilaloa hadn't given up yet, at least. And here came Joachim, splashing and grunting out of the ocean—that meant everybody was off the boat.

He saw that the Nomads were moving, and fell into their shadowy line. Nicki, behind him, held tight to his belt. Ilaloa must be taking them up now, past the island's guardians. But the Alori—

He looked down, but it was into a well of blackness. The Alori would be after them, yes—but in this wind, their gases and probably their stinging insects were useless. It would be hand-to-hand, down there at the end of the line, as Joachim and a few others fought a savage rear-guard action. Trevelyan cursed, wanting to go down and help, but the trail was too narrow, too slippery.

They came up on the heights of the island. It was overgrown with brush and wind-gnarled trees, vague in the shaking dark. But he saw thorns on flexible vines, coiled about the trunks, and thought he glimpsed eyes. He didn't know just what kind of watchers they were, but Ilaloa had commanded them to stay their attack.

Running, slipping on wet rock and crashing into half-seen boughs, he went with the Nomads through that abatis of woods. It was a short, gasping dash, and at its end the trees opened and he saw the boats.

They stood clustered as if ready to leap, spearheads poised at infinity, moonlight icy-gray on their sides. Sean was already at one of them, groping after the switch in the landing braces. He yanked it down. Under the screech of wind, Trevelyan heard the motor start up, whining. The airlock opened and the gangway ladder came down and it was nightmarishly slow.

Swinging about, Trevelyan saw the last of the Nomads burst into the clearing, Joachim bringing up the rear. They ran for the ladder as if all hell were at their heels. One by one swiftly but with some degree of order, they scampered up into the boat. He sent Sean, Ilaloa and Nicki up, and waited.

The Alori spilled out into the meadow, running hard. Joachim motioned Trevelyan up, then followed him, facing backwards. Esperero—he recognized that handsome face now—climbed in pursuit, his fellows behind him.

The captain paused near the airlock, lifting one booted foot. He had to shout to be heard, but there was an immense calm in him: "Any closer, lad, and you get your teeth bashed in."

Esperero paused. There was a sudden strangeness in the answer—pity? sorrow? "Why do you flee thus? We would not harm you. We would be your friends."

"That," said Joachim, "is just the trouble, I think."

Esperero nodded, slowly. A crooked grin twisted face. "You have a gesture, you humans," he said. "May I shake your hand?"

"Hm?" Joachim braced himself. It might be a trick, only it was hard to see what could be gained by capturing him alone. "All right. Sure." Joachim reached down. Esperero's hand was small and supple, with a warm strength, in his own clasp.

"Goodbye, my friend," said the Alorian.

He released Joachim and descended the ladder. The Nomad stared after him, then shrugged and went on up. Trevelyan pushed a button and the ladder was drawn in as the outer door whined shut. The wind's noise dimmed and silence came down like a falling moon. He locked the motor; the boat could only be opened from the inside now.

Ilaloa was standing there, too, wet and cold in the bleak white light. Her eyes were wide with a reborn fear. "Quickly," she said. "Be off, fast. There are the other boats, and they can be flown too. And they have guns!"

Joachim sprang to the nearest viewscreen, but he would see only darkness and flying clouds. He threw the intercom switch. "Emergency stations! Battle stations! And take off!"

It wasn't a normally organized crew, but the men all had some training. Boots clanged on metal as they ran for action posts. There were guns and missile tubes in the gliding fins and just above the gravity drive cones, and one heavy cannon in the nose. Joachim stayed at the centrally located airlock; Trevelyan whirled and went up the gravity shaft to the bows. Ilaloa didn't follow him, though Sean was pilot. She remained with the captain, drawing herself into a corner as if she wanted to be invisible.

Trevelyan glimpsed Nicki in one of the bunkrooms as he fell upward, and hailed her. She answered with a wave. She was helping care for one of the woman, hurt in their shipwreck land-fall. Emerging in the bow chamber, he saw Sean in the pilot chair, looking out the forward viewscreen as his fingers danced across studs and switches. The Nomad's tousled hair turned with laughter toward him. "Good man, Micah! Can you handle one of those big friends?"

"Yes, sure. But get us off the ground. Sean!" Trevelyan jumped into the gun-tender's seat. The Long John was automatically loaded and fired, but it took two men to direct the robots. Petroff Dushan was the other one; his dripping, flame-colored beard brushed the gleaming control panel. Kogama Iwao was in the co-pilot's chair, and Ferenczi sat in the background.

"I'll get her off in good time," Sean said.

It was strange, thought Trevelyan, that utter happiness should make a man so reckless of death.

The boat trembled. Sean took her up so smoothly that for an instant Trevelyan didn't realize they were headed skyward. Skyward, outward, starward—the words were a song within him.

They didn't have figures for the *Peregrine's* orbit, but she wouldn't be hard to find and board. And after that—

"They're firing, Sean," said Kogama.

Sean looked at the detector dials. The craft lurched a bit from a near miss, exploded by her own counterfire. "Yeah," he said. "And—oh, oh!" He spoke into the intercom. "Pilot to captain. They're taking another of the boats after us. Neutrino emission."

"Just let me focus my screen," answered Joachim. "Uh-huh, I see it now. Brethren, this is not a good thing."

Sean reached out and worked the dials of his

own auxiliary screen until it showed the ground below. That was a huge black circle, falling away as they climbed for heaven. The moonlight picked out steel below them, rising.

"Can we give 'em the slip?" asked Ferenczi.

"No," said Sean. "They're coming too fast. We'd better swing around so we can use our heavy stuff."

Joachim's voice rattled over the intercom: "Captain to crew. Captain to crew. Looks like a fight. Strap in."

The boat didn't have internal gravity fields, except for the shaft. Trevelyan buckled the webbing about himself and looked out into a night of rushing wind. His hands moved along the polished deadlines of the Long John's controls. *I had hoped we could get away without this,* he thought.

His head swooped as Sean brought the boat around. They slanted over the planet's surface, seeking to use the advantage of height. The other boat climbed steeply toward them. Trevelyan saw flame as the intercepted shells blew up. Once a shrapnel burst struck the hull near the bows, and it rang like a great gong.

"His piloting stinks," said Sean. "This'll be easy."

"Do we have to do it?" Surprisingly, it was Ferenczi who said that. "Can't we just outrun him?"

"And be gunned down from behind? If that lunatic doesn't know when he's beaten, he'll have to be shown." The hardness died in Sean's voice and he bit his lip. "But I hate to do this!"

Esperero, thought Trevelyan grayly, *is my friend.*

For a moment the philosophy of a lifetime buckled. *How long will we have to accept the world as it is? How long will we have to stand by with empty hands and see injustice done?*

The Nomad boat dived close, swooping on her enemy like a hawk. The Alorian pilot tried to evade them, swerving clumsily aside. Sean passed within meters of the other, and everything his boat had cut loose as he rushed by. Fire lanced over the sky and the Alorian boat went down in a hot rain of metal.

It wasn't right! They shouldn't have died that way!

The Nomads turned upward again; Trevelyan saw that they had crossed the edge of night. The sun was low in the east, shadows long across a forest world that glittered with dew.

"We're away." Suddenly Sean threw back his head and laughed. "We're away and free again!"

Trevelyan heard a shout over the intercom—Joachim's bull roar, broken in the middle. After it came a great howling of wind.

"What the hell—?" Sean bent over his mike. "What's wrong, Skipper?"

The wind hooted. There was a cold draft up the gravity tube. "I'll go," said Trevelyan. His voice seemed as if it came from outside himself. "I'll go find out what it is."

Trevelyan threw off the safety webbing, and ran across the deck, two steps to the shaft and then down the beam like a dead leaf falling in England's

October. He heard Joachim over the loudspeakers: "It's all right. Just a little accident. Captain to crew, remain at battle posts."

Trevelyan emerged in the airlock vestibule. The outer door was open to a sky that seemed infinitely blue. Joachim stood by the chamber with his clothes whipping about a stooped form. The battered homely face turned to him, fighting to keep itself steady. Joachim was crying. He didn't know how; he wept so heavily and awkwardly that it was as if it would shake his body apart. "How'll I tell him, Micah? How'll I tell the lad?"

"She jumped?"

"I was busy at the screen, watching. I saw the boat blow up, and stood there for a minute after. Then I heard the airlock motor start. The door was open a little bit, and Ilaloa stood there. I ran to grab her, but the door opened just enough more for her to go out."

Joachim shook his head. "But how am I going to tell Sean?"

Trevelyan didn't answer. He thought of Ilaloa, falling through the sky down to her forest, and wondered what she had been thinking of in that time. He thumbed the switch, and the door closed.

Trevelyan Micah straightened himself and laid a hand on Joachim's shoulder. "It's all right," he said. "There's more to Sean than you know. But let's not tell him just yet."

The sky darkened around them and the stars came forth.

POUL ANDERSON

48923	**The Long Way Home**	$1.95
51904	**The Man Who Counts**	$1.95
57451	**The Night Face**	$1.95
65954	**The Peregrine**	$1.95
69770	**Question and Answer**	$1.50
91706	**World Without Stars**	$1.50
91056	**The Worlds of Poul Anderson**	$1.95
	THE SAGA OF DOMINIC FLANDRY	
20724	**Ensign Flandry**	$1.95
24071	**Flandry of Terra**	$1.95

Available wherever paperbacks are sold or use this coupon.

Ace Science Fiction, Book Mailing Service,
Box 690, Rockville Centre, N.Y. 11571

Please send me titles checked above.

I enclose $ . . . . Add 50¢ handling fee per copy.

Name . . . .

Address . . . .

City . . . . State . . . . Zip . . . .

Ursula K. Le Guin

10704	**City of Illusion**	$1.95
47805	**Left Hand of Darkness**	$1.95
66956	**Planet of Exile**	$1.95
73294	**Rocannon's World**	$1.95